RED AND WHITE

Red and White

Stories of Poland

Mark Lewandowski

Cover design by Jacob Arms

Published by Serving House Books
William K. Lawrence, Editor in Chief
Lawrence Landing Company
Raleigh, North Carolina 27609
United States of America
www.servinghousebooks.com

Serving House Books is a proud member of

Independent Book Publishers Association
 and
Community of Literary Magazines and Presses

CONTENTS

For Katie

Acknowledgements:

The New Economy, *Ginosko Literary Journal*
Past Perfect, *Rain Crow*
The Silent Fall, *The Florida Review*
Beer Money, *The Louisville Review*
The Widower, *Hamilton Stone Review*
Amber, *Oyez Review*
Shallow Grave, *Clackamas Literary Review*
Thirst, *Main Street Rag*

Thank you to Indiana State University for the sabbaticals that helped to make this book possible. And to my friends and students in Biala Podlaska, Poland: you will forever be in my heart.

THE NEW ECONOMY

An incidental touch. Anya's pinky lightly brushing her wrist. The tingle slowly traveling up Renata's arm. The sensation opening into a magnificent fall day. The two traipsing through the linden trees hunting for the season's last mushrooms. A reddened leaf floating and floating before landing in Renata's basket…

Jarred. Yanked from the past. Not so much by a sound, but a slight movement in the earth, a faint concussion. Not every bomb dropped from every Messerschmitt found its target or detonated. That's what it felt like, that same reverberation in her bones from fifty years earlier: 250 kilos of dead weight thunking into a distant field. Renata shook her head and looked down. The water had long ago filled the kettle. She turned off the faucet.

"Ridiculous."

Something creaked outside, and then something banged. She wondered if the barn door opened in the night. Henryk roused his old self from the pile of blankets near the front door and barked away, setting the cocks to crowing and the chickens to squawking. Unmilked and unfed Emilia wouldn't get far, but Renata left the kettle and the bread rising on the counter, changed slippers for Wellingtons and scurried outside.

"With me," she commanded Henryk, who whined, and then pawed at the threshold before slumping after her. The early light slithered through the trees and tip-toed on the watering pond. Sure enough the barn door was open. Henryk, more lively now, trotted over, growling at the darkness seeping from the barn. Renata, though, saw something down by water's edge, a big lump. Heard it, too. The lump was snoring.

"Oh, Jesus," she said. "Emilia, is it." Yes, her milk cow, on her side, snout a few centimeters in the water, the gusts from her nostrils blowing ripples. Renata gave her a good shove with both palms.

"Up now, beast!"

The cow heaved a sigh and continued to blubber into the water. Renata pressed her ear to Emilia's side; the heartbeat sounded normal, and no obstruction gurgled in her gut. Meanwhile, Henryk went from growling to excited yipping. The shadows from the barn had cut away his body. There was just his disembodied tail wagging in the dawn's light.

"Have you come for a visit, my love?" Renata asked the sky.

When she reached the barn Henryk spun and slipped between her legs. Renata felt for the lantern and searched the pockets on her coveralls for a match.

Something was stirring in the barn. A cat? A hare? No. Something bigger. She primed the lantern, flicked the match head with a thumbnail, and lit the mantel.

"Hello? No games now. I haven't had my tea," she said, probing the dark with the lantern's glare.

To the left her Polski Fiat, covered with a blue plastic tarp, looked untouched. The pitchforks and shovels still hung from the back wall. The milking stool and buckets, all there. The door to Emilia's stall, though, was open. The leather strap used to keep it shut hung loose, but intact.

She stepped into the stall, lantern held high. She didn't see anything immediately, not until she lowered the light.

In the corner. What was it? A man? A boy? Naked, apparently, and white. Like unpolished marble. Renata thought back to the old stone kings on their coffins in Cracow's cathedral. Anya had taken her there once. So long ago, it seemed. This thing, this creature in her milk cow's stall, looked like that, one of those kings, but only if someone had stripped it of robe, of crown, of sword and orb, peeled it from the coffin and tossed the limp bag of a body into the corner.

Renata stepped closer and held the light above the thing's face. Its eyes popped open, sending up a fine spray of dust. A big, brilliant green, the eyes were. Electric, even. Like Christmas lights. The figure pulled itself into a seated position and squeezed tighter into the corner of the stall. Henryk remained behind Renata's legs and whined.

"Huh," she said. "And who might you be, and what did you do to Emilia?"

The manboy of marble blinked rapidly, sending out more dust. He mumbled something, but Renata couldn't understand it.

"I can't hear you," she said.

The manboy slithered across the stall and bowed, those green eyes looking up to her. It spoke again, firing off a barrage of guttural, sometimes squeaky sounds. It wasn't Polish or Russian or Ukrainian or German or Yiddish. Probably not English or French or whatever else.

Maybe the poor thing was slow. There was a smell, now that she thought of it. She knelt to take a big whiff. What was that, underneath the hay and manure? Alcohol? Just a drunk then? But how did he end up in her barn? The nearest bar was ten kilometers away. She stood and searched the stall. No empties.

"Men...Well, you can sleep it off, but be on your way afterwards."

It was getting lighter out. She extinguished the lantern and went to check on Emilia.

"To me, Henryk."

The old dog made it to the barn door, where it dropped to his haunches and looked back towards the stall. Emilia still snored away. Before Renata reached her, the cow rolled over on her back and shimmied, for a moment all four feet straight in the air and shaking like flag poles in a heavy wind before she flopped over to her other side, on impact blasting out a loud and odiferous fart.

"Oh, Jesus," Renata said, stepping back.

Emilia blinked and licked her lips.

Renata looked past the cow, over the watering pond and into the shadowed trees. Something wasn't right. She felt it.

She reached down and patted Emilia.

"You're fine for now, and I need my tea."

The manboy, the creature, that thing from the cow stall, now stood shivering out in the open as Henryk circled him, play barking and snipping at his heels. As Renata approached he wouldn't look her in the eye. He was a small, scrawny thing, and wore no clothes, except underwear, it looked like, though he covered his crotch with his hands. He was caked in something and was starting to crack. There was a bushy head of black hair, she could see now, and full brows.

"I'll have no drunks in my house," Renata said. "Touch your nose."

He still wouldn't look at her, not into she snapped her fingers inches from his face.

"Like this."

She stepped back and extended her left her arm to her side before slowly bringing her a fingertip to her nose, then did the same with her right. The man, the boy, the whatever, looked down at Henryk who panted in response.

Renata again snapped her fingers.

"He's not going to help you," she said, arching an eyebrow.

Now he did as commanded. Satisfied, Renata grabbed his arm and pulled him towards the front door.

"A stranger in the house is like God in the house, as Grandmama used to say. We'll see about that."

...

She had a big tub, from before the war, she reckoned. It had come with the house. In the time it took to fill, she was able to get the bread in the oven, to collect the eggs and feed the chickens, to slice the cheese, the ham, the tomato and cucumber, and set the table. When was the last time she had laid out a spread for a guest? Since Father Marek? Or her neighbors Mikhail and Ludmila? She couldn't remember. She missed it though, the company.

In the bathroom the tub was full. The manboy stood guard next to it, his hands still covering his crotch. Given the crumbles and dust left on the seat it was clear he had least used the toilet. Now, looking at him closely under the light she realized he was encased in mud and clay.

"Go on," she said, pointing to the tub. "You're not sitting at my table in that state."

He looked down at the floor. Dried bits dropped from his head.

"Ridiculous," she said, and turned around.

She waited for him to get into the tub, but not for long. As a nurse, back when she still worked, first at a hospital in Warsaw and later at a country clinic, she'd dealt with far larger, and more stubborn patients. She turned quickly, scooped him up in her arms and dropped him into the steaming bath. He squealed but didn't resist. Renata rolled up a sleeve and thrust her hand into the scolding water, under his legs. Those big green eyes of his widened even more when she pulled off his underwear, and without looking, flung them over her shoulder; they splatted right in the center of the hand sink.

"I'll find you some clothes," she said, handing him a rough sponge.

She thought for a moment for what might fit the manboy. She had some old coveralls an itinerant worker had left behind. They'd been patched in multiple places and the front zipper was broken, but they were clean. There were work shirts, too. Even some underwear of her own, from back when lady things weren't so easy to buy in Poland. She sat at the table and sipped her tea. She didn't hear much splashing.

"I have things to do," she shouted. Though she really didn't.

After a couple minutes she barged back into the bathroom. Her guest had made some headway, but now he was just splotchy.

"Ridiculous." She knelt and grabbed the sponge. He squirmed and grunted as she scraped at his back and shoulders. That done, she pulled him back by the hair and went to work on the front, first his chest and arms. Now she could see he was actually quite hairy. Older than she had reckoned. She rubbed more soap into the sponge and did his legs and thighs. He squirmed less, became even too quiet. Renata, her face just centimeters away, looked down.

There was his *ptak*, unsheathed and pink, poking eel-like out of the mucky water.

She stopped then. And remembered.

How many years ago? She was so young...Anya had brought a man home, to their apartment in Warsaw. A man. Renata locked herself in the bathroom and cried and cried while Anya and the man drank vodka in the kitchen. So stupid, really. Anya wanted a child. So did Renata. This was the only way. But still. A man in their bed?

Soon Anya and the man left the kitchen and shuffled towards the bedroom. Renata snuck out of the bathroom and pressed her ear to the bedroom door. She heard mumbling and murmuring and the unzipping of clothes and then a chuckle, and a laugh, and at last Anya, that sweet woman, began cackling hysterically.

Through the door she heard the man tumble to the floor and she hurried away to the kitchen and pretended to read the back of the vodka bottle. With Anya's laughter echoing behind him the man, red-faced and fuming, stumbled through the flat, out the front door and down the dark stairwell, never to be seen again.

So there were no children.

Renata sighed.

The manboy-she'd have to find out his name-was still in the bath, and there, still, was his *ptak*. She flicked the tip with her finger. Hard. He yelped and flipped to his side, looking back at her with wounded eyes.

"It's okay," she said quietly. She grew gentle then. She squeezed some shampoo onto his head and lathered it into his thick hair. She cooed as she massaged his scalp. This seemed to calm him. It took some time to get all the grit from his head, but eventually it was done. She handed him her thickest towel, pointed to the clothes, and went to the kitchen to scramble the eggs with fresh chives and a dash of cream.

At first he stood nervously in the doorway. He did look silly, Renata admitted. The coveralls were too big for him; he had to roll up the legs just to walk. Eventually, though, when it was clear the spread on the table was for him, he sat and started shoveling it in.

"Slowly!" Renata said, touching his hand. "You'll get sick."

He just kept eating, which made her happy despite herself. He wouldn't touch the ham, though, even after she nudged the plate toward him.

"Ham is good," she said. She speared a slice and tried to put it on his plate but he stopped it with his hand.

He was dark, darker than most Slavs. Jewish? No. She'd seen him. All of him. Maybe Tarter.

"Renata," she said, touching her chest. "Re-na-ta." She then pointed to him. "You?"

He'd just chugged half a glass of milk and now had a white mustache and some drops on the tip of his nose.

"Ah," he said. "Fattah. Fat-tah."

He piled more cucumber and cheese on a slice of still warm bread and stuffed it into his mouth.

Fattah, Renata thought. Fattah?

She left him to his food and skipped to the main room. Even though there was a television in there, it was more of a library, with cases overflowing with journals, magazines and books, especially novels, including the westerns Anya loved so, every Louis L'Amour and Zane Grey she could find in translation, as well as all the Russian and Polish classics. Above the cases hung framed collections of some of the awards and accolades, including the Cross of the Brave, and other ribbons and testimonials Anya had received from the Home Army and the Party and the Sejm. Framed photos, too. Even some from the war of Anya and Renata, both in jerry-rigged uniforms, snapped and developed, somehow, someway, by the nine-year old son of a murdered wedding photographer.

While she scanned the shelves for the atlas, Fattah had sidled up to her so quietly her heart leapt.

"You're a sneaky little bugger, aren't you?"

He still had some bread with him and chewed while he looked at the photos on the desk. There was Anya with President Walesa, and another of both Anya and Renata with Pope John Paul II. Even one with General Jarulzelski on the eve of Martial Law.

The largest, though, was the last taken of Anya. She was bare-chested, but the angry scar that had replaced her left breast was hidden by the stock of the old Gewehr 24 liberated from the first Hitlerite she had garroted. For the picture she had removed the sun hat from her bald head, and even though her face had lost all its roundness she still struck Renata as the Amazonian who clawed her way through the war, and later, up the ladder of Poland's male-dominated political machine.

She took up the framed photo and held it to her chest.

"We argued that day," she said. "She didn't want to go back to the hospital. 'But maybe this time it'll take, I said.'"

She knew Fattah didn't understand, but she kept talking, and he looked at here with those bright green eyes as if he actually could.

"Who could blame her? Every time she came back from Warsaw there was less of her. First her muscles, then her hair, then one breast."

She placed the picture back carefully on the desk, wiping away a bit of dust from the brass frame. There, right above the typewriter, nestled the atlas.

"Ridiculous. I was looking right at it."

She pulled it out. It wasn't more than ten years old, but still out of date. In it Germany was two countries, Czechoslovakia just one. On the page for Poland she found where they were: south of Bialystok, a stone's throw from the River Bug, the border with Belarus.

"Renata, here," she said. "Fattah? Poland?"

He shook his head. She turned to the page encompassing all of Eastern Europe. Still he shook his head. He spun the book, flipped a few pages and pointed.

"Afghanistan?" Renata asked.

Fattah put his hand on his heart and sighed.

"Huh," she said.

Fattah finished off his bread.

Outside, there was a commotion.

"For heaven's sake! Emilia!"

On her way out she tripped over Henryk, who had dragged his empty food bowl into the hallway and dropped his head into it.

"My word!" Renata said. She filled the bowl with kibble and out of guilt covered the mound with the ham her visitor refused. What a day, she thought, what a day.

Outside, the milk cow had managed to get to her feet and slowly lumbered back to the barn. The sun arched above the tree line. Now Renata could see the far edge of the watering pond clearly. The level had risen over night.

Really? A small channel had opened on the edge nearest the woods and water sluiced through it. Now she noticed the pond's shore had inched closer to the house. What? Had Emilia misjudged the edge? Slipped?

Only occasionally, after the heaviest sustained rain, had this happened. It hadn't rained in nearly a week. How was this possible?

"Fattah?"

He had followed her outside, he thought, but now he was nowhere to be seen.

"Men," she mumbled.

On the far side of the pond, at the base of a large ash tree, a large puddle had formed. But now, no more water seemed to be leaking from the pond.

"I'm losing my mind, I am…"

Fattah must have something to do with this, she thought. My pond. Emilia. She'd find out, she would. She hoofed it back up to the yard in time to see a large air bubble form in the middle of the pond. It stretched above the surface—a good foot at least—before collapsing, sending a small wave back over the edge and into the woods.

"Fattah!"

Nothing.

She poked her head in the house and called but got no answer. Then she heard the unmistakable sound of milk spraying into a bucket. In the barn there was Fattah, happily squatted under Emilia, expertly draining her udder. Her cow looked at her and mooed softly, apparently not at all alarmed by this strange man's hands on her.

"Well, now."

Time to take stock. Her cow had tipped over for no apparent reason. A strange man, from Afghanistan, of all places, appeared out of nowhere, like he was dropped from the sky. No angel wings, though. Nor car, clothes, or identification. Maybe he swam across the river? But what was he doing in Belarus? Her watering pond had grown in volume, and if that air bubble was any indication, something was feeding it from underground. All these things must be connected, though she couldn't figure out how. Phone calls could be placed. To the police.

Or to certain numbers in Warsaw.

Someone would come and take him away, and she could go about her day. There were things to do, surely. Perhaps a rummage at the Russian market in Bialystok. Or a film at the theater.

The funeral was 741 days ago. Renata had yet to go back to work at the clinic. Anya tried to make her promise she would. After. Renata reasoned if she couldn't care for the love of her life, couldn't stop what was happening, what good was she to anyone else?

Instead, she became a master at puttering away the hours of the day.

Yes, she could make a call, and someone would take Fattah away and she could get back to...things.

"Emilia doesn't seem to mind you," she called out.

Milk he certainly could, but Fattah somehow managed to dump the entire bucket. No matter. There was plenty in the refrigerator. Likely perturbed by his clumsiness, he next attacked the weeds in the vegetable garden. He quickly found other chores as well, like changing the hay in the cow stall, strengthening the patch in the chicken coop, and clambering up to the roof of the house to clear the gutters.

It was nice, Renata had to admit. She wasn't always on top of things. Sometimes she forgot to collect the eggs, and the fall after the funeral she let the vegetables rot in the fields and the apples and pears drop, brown and shrunken, to the early snow. The farm had been more of a pastoral fantasy, even before Anya died. They'd bought it as a weekend getaway in '84, a dacha where they could grow fresh produce. Only after Anya left the Sejm did they sell the apartment in Warsaw to live here permanently. This was the place they were to grow old together. Even though they bought Emilia and a dozen chickens, they needn't depend on the farm financially. After the war Anya, just five years her senior, had officially adopted Renata. And now, even after Anya's death, monthly deposits were made to her bank account, more than what the official state pension could account for. On her death bed Anya had assured her she would be taken care of.

"Don't worry about it, Little Mole," she whispered, touching Renata's cheek with fingers light as her voice. "Haven't I always protected you?"

Fattah hammered at something outside. Renata looked down at the phone and absently scratched the back of her neck. No, she wouldn't call the police, or Warsaw, at least not yet. There was the Afghan embassy. They'd have a dictionary, at least.

But. What if. What if Fattah was some kind of fugitive? Would they be looking for him? Afghanistan had become a lawless place, she'd read, after the Soviets left with tails between their legs. Why didn't she let Anya buy them that computer? There was something called the World Wide Web, she heard. You could find things.

Renata shrugged. Give it a few days. Maybe he'd be gone by then, as quickly and silently as he arrived. That prospect saddened her for some reason. Just in case, though, she lifted the top of the convertible couch in the library and rummaged through the bedding and pillows stored there. They were clean, but the wind would blow some freshness into them. Outside she set the feather pillow under a sun beam and pinned the sheets to the line. Back inside she scrubbed the dried gunk from Fattah's underwear before dropping them into the washer. Soon it would be lunch time. What besides pork would a Muslim not eat? Potato cutlet would be safe. Eventually she'd have to do some shopping, but for now there was plenty. The house came with its own "Priest Hole," as the English call them, though during the war the family who owned the farm hid partisans in there, or maybe Jews. Both Germans and Russians had requisitioned the building, which is how it had remained intact so close to areas of battle. It was rumored in the surrounding areas that when a Polish family once again took over the farm in 1946, they found two skeletons down there: one of an adult, one of a child, their intertwined bones swaddled in rotted clothing. Supposedly, they'd silently starved to death waiting for the Germans and/or the Russians to leave the premises.

Renata accessed the Priest Hole by pushing a button hidden on the floor beneath the base of a lamp. A bookcase slid behind the couch, and steep stairs led down into what was essentially a concrete bunker. These days Renata used it mainly for a root cellar, though Anya had provisioned it years earlier with water, canned goods, cots and blankets, even a two-way radio "in case the Americans invade." A wall locker held Anya's Gewehr, Renata's Karabinek, three handguns, including a Luger, and ammunition for all, as well as various blades. Whether out of habit or buried worry, the women had kept the weapons clean and oiled.

She slipped the Luger from its peg.

"Ridiculous."

Still, she didn't put it back. She couldn't explain why. Other than Fattah's appearance wasn't, well, normal. She slipped the case from the handle and filled it with 9 mm bullets. She dropped the gun into the pouch in front of her coveralls, on her way upstairs taking a packet of dried mushrooms and a jar of green beans.

In the bedroom she could hear Fattah clambering on the roof. A broken tree limb with a smattering of dead leaves sailed past the window. Renata slid the Luger under Anya's pillow, then went to the kitchen to soak the mushrooms.

...

Fattah devoured everything Renata set in front of him: the chicken soup, buttered bread, the potato cutlets with mushroom sauce, the leek salad, and two large glasses of raspberry compote. Even half of a packaged German loaf cake. After, eyes droopy, he smoothed his napkin and penciled what she assumed was his family. Stick figured wife, two girls, and what might've been three cats. Renata laughed. And then teared up.

As it turned out, Fattah did seem to understand some Russian. A few words here and there, so she switched from Polish and told her guest about the first real happy day of her life, even though he probably couldn't follow it completely.

It was right after the Hitlerites left Warsaw, making their way back through the wasteland they had created, to their last stand in Berlin, just before the Russians crossed from the eastern banks of the Vistula. Someone had miraculously found a working projector and an American film, a Charlie Chaplan one, and Anya and Renata and a smattering of other survivors of the Uprising, those fortunate enough to evade capture, including children and the elderly, bodies diminished from hunger and disease, crouched in a theater, roof ripped from the walls, and watched it, over and over again, their high-pitched laughter bouncing off the smoldering ruins of their beloved city. Even after the stars began to disappear in the morning light, they rewound it and rewatched until not one drop of gasoline remained in the generator.

The crowd broke up then to scrounge for breakfast. Near what remained of Saxon Garden Renata spotted a scrawny cat mewing in a bomb crater. Anya pounced, grabbed it by the neck and shattered its temple with the butt-end of her bayonet. Skinning that cat Anya started laughing again as she recounted Chaplan eating his shoe. With the cat spitted and roasting over a coal fire, she finally stopped, if only to eat. They sat elbow to elbow in the bowels of the crater, ripping at the stringy meat and sucking on the bones. After slurping from a shallow puddle they flipped onto their backs and looked up at the promising blue sky.

"So what did you think of breakfast?" Anya asked.

"Tasted like a shoe."

That only got her going again, and Renata started in as well. For who knows how long they laughed until Anya hiccupped.

"You brat," she said. "I pissed myself!" She grabbed Renata by the neck and pressed her greasy lips to hers.

The first kiss. Just fourteen years old, Renata knew then that this woman, this savior, who pulled her from the rubble of her family's apartment block, would be so much, much more than the mother figure she had clung to for five years.

Oh how her mind wandered these days. Only into the past, though. No longer about what could be. Just memories unspooling like an old broken film.

Fattah was asleep. Upright in his chair. Renata gently shook him awake and led him to the library, where she stripped him of coveralls and tucked him into bed. He began to snore even before she could close the curtains against the mid-afternoon sun.

...

The next morning Henryk licked her awake. He only did that when she overslept. Sure enough the sun was already up.

"Day 742," she said, wiping sleep dust from her eyelids.

"Oh, right. Fattah. Slept right through dinner, he did. Must be starving."

The table, however, was already set for her. He'd even managed to make a type of flat bread. She looked out the window above the sink. Her houseguest was out there scything the tall grass. She knocked on the window. When he looked up she waved and smiled.

The bread was delicious. She'd have to ask him how to make it. After she finished she poured milk into a pot and squeezed three lemons into it. Once the milk curdled she'd wrap it in cheese cloth and hang it from the faucet to drain; the soft cheese would be excellent on Fattah's bread. Maybe some honey on top.

As she bathed she thought of driving into Bialystok. The new German supermarket there might have lamb chops. That would take all morning, though, and she wasn't sure if Fattah would be comfortable going with her or staying behind for so long. Instead, she packed up some snares and a catch pole.

He was still cutting the grass—she hadn't done it in over a year.

"I go down there," she said, gesturing beyond the vegetable garden.

He mouthed something and pointed to himself.

She shook her head. "No, I go. Ducks." She showed him the catch pole. "Quack, quack!" She pointed to him with one hand and then held up a palm. "You stay. I won't be long."

He looked first beyond the garden, and then back in the opposite direction, towards the long road that ended at her house.

Was he nervous, she wondered? Did he plan on leaving?

"You come then," she said, waving him forward.

He smiled but shook his head and started back on the grass, whistling that tune again.

Henryk followed her, though sometimes she had to stop and wait for him to catch up. The duck pond was a good fifteen-minute walk, around a dense grove of trees that thrust into her fields. Sure enough four ducks splashed happily in the water. Before she looped one, she set the snares; wild hare often watered here. Fattah might like the terrine she made with them; Anya certainly did. She found some late season black raspberries, too. She filled a plastic shopping bag with them, then looped a duck before heading back. Again she often had to wait on Henryk, but she was in too good a mood to be cross with him; he couldn't help it, the old thing.

They eventually rounded the grove. Fattah was no longer working on the grass, but he had left the scythe. Renata stopped. Though the duck had been calm up to this point, it started to thrash in the bag. Henryk whimpered.

"Ssssh."

She took a few more steps, just until she could see around the corner of the house, between the barn and chicken coop. An unfamiliar vehicle was there. A white one. Only the front was visible, since the barn blocked the back end. Might be a small delivery van. Maybe she had no reason to think the worst, that Fattah, and by extension herself, were in danger here, but she trusted her instincts. She'd survived the war, hadn't she, and not always with Anya's help. Fattah wouldn't have left a tool in the field. This is why she had loaded the Luger. Fat lot of good, though; it was still under the pillow.

She tipped the duck out of the bag and kicked it back towards the pond. Henryk immediately loped after it. Renata crept up to the barn. No one was in sight, but then someone coughed and smoke streamed over the vehicle. She continued behind the building and peaked around the corner. A man. In a bright baby blue tracksuit. He had his back to her, smoking and looking towards her house. It was a delivery van all right, with Belarussian plates. The back was open; Fattah, bound and gagged, lay inside. He had been stripped naked. Even from this distance she could see that one eye was swollen shut.

There had been so many like that in the war. Beaten and bloodied, men, boys, old women, young women, thrown into the back of trucks and kept alive just for the trip to the countryside where'd they be summarily shot and dumped into shallow ditches.

She turned and considered the catch pole. The wire loop was strong, but was it big enough to get over Tracksuit's head? And quickly? She doubted it.

She'd have to improvise. She set down the catch pole and bag of raspberries and quietly turned the corner. Fattah raised his head. Renata pursed her lips and pressed them with her pointer finger.

She slowly made her way to the barn's entrance. A lightness had kicked in. She wasn't nervous, nor worried that the strange man in the tracksuit would turn. Just like fifty years ago, right before she drove the needle-pointed knife up under the rib cage of her first kill.

No knife this time. No matter. She reached into the barn and grabbed the first weapon at hand: a garden spade. With the back of Tracksuit still facing her, she pulled down her sun hat and stooped over. Like a walking stick she held the spade with both hands and shook them as if palsied. Shuffling now, she inched forward and cleared her throat.

Tracksuit finally turned.

"Well, ah, hello, Granny!" he said in Russian.

"I see you have him," she said.

"Ah, this?" he said, tapping cigarette ash onto Fattah's head.

"I thought he was going to kill me," she croaked out, still shuffling forward.

"Our little boy? We are, ah, sorry about that."

The man now leaned back against the van, his right foot bent back and flat against the bumper.

Idiot, Renata thought. So sure of himself. It's the scared ones you had to worry about. They're unpredictable.

Still moving. Closer now.

"You'll have to forgive my brother," Tracksuit said. "He's, ahhh, using your facilities? I hope he, ah, doesn't destroy anything? We'll compensate you, if so. Plus whatever our little digger cost you. My brother. His bowels are always giving him problems. He fancies himself, ahhh, a vegetarian? But the man doesn't like vegetables? So it's all, just bread and-"

Renata slammed the spade's blade down on the crown of his head, dropping him like a sack of turnips. What a nice sound, she thought. A good, clean thud. He'd be out for a while. She dragged him to the right of the vehicle, out of sight from the front door of her house. Fattah started squirming and struggling over the gag.

"Shhh!" Renata implored, holding up a palm. "One more?" she whispered, holding up a finger.

Fattah nodded as best he could.

She took up the spade once again and held it, blade to the ground. Like before she stooped over and pulled down the lip of the hat's brim, not so much though that she couldn't keep one eye on the front door.

The man who came out of her house was clearly a brother, an identical twin, most likely. He had the same square face, the same bulbous nose and receding hairline. Even the tracksuit matched; his, however, was cherry red.

"Hello!" he called out. "You'll have to forgive me for that, Grandmother. I couldn't even flush! Our digger has cost you enough, I'm sure, and here I go, causing you more trouble. No problem. I'm good for it."

From the front pocket of this tracksuit he pulled a wad of money—American dollars she thought—and flipped individual bills into the air as he walked, leaving behind a trail.

"My good brother tells me I have to cut down on the cheese, but I love it so. Camembert, Provolone, Gouda, even the Polish stuff I'll gobble up, so I took some medicine for, well, you know, my issues. The box promised 'easy relief,' but I have to tell—"

Down came the spade. He dropped just as easily as his brother. What a rush!

Adrenaline still surging, Renata slipped off Fattah's gag. He spit out a bloody tooth.

"Whore!" she shouted, taking up the spade once again. Before she could swing at Red Tracksuit's head--that big, meaty croquet ball at her feet--Fattah tumbled out of the van. His hands were tied behind his back, but still he managed to wrap his skinny body around Renata's legs.

"No No No!" he cried in Russian, shaking his swollen head.

Renata dropped the spade.

"Ridiculous," she said. "All right. Get off me now. I don't know who these two characters are, but they're not worth your bother, I assure you."

She was able to untie Fattah without the help of a knife. His clothes she found in a pile near the driver's seat in the van. While he dressed, she went to the barn. She kept a stock of livestock tranquilizers there. Fattah's one good eye grew wide when she came back with the large hypodermic.

"Don't worry," she said. "Only to sleep." She titled her head and pretended to snore.

After pumping healthy doses into both, she rifled through their pockets. Red Tracksuit had that wad of American bills. The first was a hundred, the rest all ones. Breath mints, keys. Not much else. Not even an Afghan-Russian dictionary. She found their passports in the glove compartment, as well an old Makarov. Loaded. She pocketed the gun and left the rest. She had hoped for some identification for Fattah.

Henryk had made his way back and was now sniffing Blue Tracksuit.

"What am I to do with these lumps? Can't just leave them."

So she and Fattah rolled them up in horse blankets and bound them in packing tape.

Now what? She needed help.

Mikhail. He and Ludmila were caretakers of the park bordering Renata's property. In order to get to her house—by car, at least—you had to pass theirs. Perhaps it was no surprise then that when she went to call, her message light was blinking. While she was picking berries and setting her snares, the white delivery van had passed Mikhail as he tended his prized chrysanthemums. He thought it odd, he said in the message, this white delivery van with Belarussian plates. She called back. He agreed to come. No questions asked.

While she waited for him, Renata tended to Fattah. The swollen part of his face was already turning purple and yellow. She dabbed at it with peroxide and butterflied the worst of the cuts. After testing his one good eye for concussion, she wrapped ice in a kitchen towel and showed how to apply it. She couldn't do much about the new gap in his teeth.

"Not too hard now," she said.

Soon, Mikhail clopped into the yard on Maria, a feisty mare who'd burst herself on Renata's pears if you let her. Guilt swept through Renata. How many winter nights had the four of them stayed up late playing Gin Rummy? Or whiled away long summer days roasting sausages over a crackling fire? She'd only had Mikhail and Ludmila over once since Anya left her. 42 days after.

"You're looking good," Renata called out from the front door.

"Honey!" Mikhail said. "Flattery will take you anywhere."

"I was talking to the horse."

"Ha!"

Mikhail was a big man, with a full, bushy beard and long hair kept black as tar with dye. He leapt from the mare and fed her a carrot from his own mouth.

"So what do we have here," he said. "Two piggies in a blanket?"

The feet of both Tracksuits stuck out. White tennis shoes. Ridiculous. Mikhail gave Red Tracksuit a good kick.

"Dead?"

"Not yet."

"Probably foot soldiers," Mikhail said. "More and more are coming over the border to do 'business.'"

"Yes."

"But not with you, Honey?"

"Not any business I'm interested in."

Mikhail arched an eyebrow. He could really get it up there, like an inverted checkmark.

Renata sighed. "Fattah!"

A moment later Henryk led him out.

"Well who's this little guy?" Mikhail asked.

Eyes on the ground, Fattah placed himself right behind Renata. She could feel his breath on her back.

"It's all right, Fattah. Mikhail is a friend." She stepped aside so Mikhail could get a look at his face, then told him the story, all the way back to her discovery of Emilia the previous morning.

"This piggie here called him a 'digger.'"

"Smuggling, then?" Mikhail asked. "Under the river?"

Renata shrugged.

Mikhail stared off into the woods.

Of course, Renata thought. A tunnel. The pond. Emilia. She drank from the pond. He probably dumped the milk on purpose, then.

"Alcohol," she said.

"What, my love?"

"Vodka, they're smuggling vodka."

"Yes, yes!" Fattah said, nodding his head, but then he moaned and pressed the ice pack against his eye. "Vodka," he whispered.

"Vodka?" Mikhail said. "Here? We bathe in the stuff! Why smuggle it in?"

Renata shrugged. "Duties? I guess they're pretty high now, right?"

"It's the new economy," Mikhail said. "What do the Americans say? Anything for a buck?"

"Ridiculous."

"You know I'd the move the sun for you, my sweet. Do you have an extra shovel?"

Why not. This was Poland. There were more people under the ground than above it. What were two more?

"Despite what they did to him, Fattah seems to care for some reason," Renata said.

"I'll take them back for you, just leave the van somewhere," Mikhail said. "I have friends in Terespol. I can cross back over by foot. No problem."

"Keep the van," Renata said.

Mikhail walked around it, nodding.

"Mercedes," he said. "Pretty new. I can get a decent price for it in Ukraine."

"You're a saint."

"Again with the flattery. I can take him, too."

"Fattah," she said, pointing to the van. "You go?"

She felt half-hearted about it. He was trouble, most certainly, but she liked having him around. She imagined something crazy, like him bringing his family from Afghanistan, even the cats, taking over the farm close by.

"Back to Belarus, maybe?" she said, gesturing, pointing. "With your friends?"

It took him a moment, but he then seemed to understand.

"No!" he shouted, shaking his head. "No!" He dropped the ice and ran back around the van. The trail of the one-dollar bills flung by Red Tracksuit still lay in the dirt. He snatched them up, even went after one a bit of wind picked up and blew around. It reminded Renata of Henryk as a young pup chasing after a butterfly.

Mikhail laughed.

Fattah came back and shoved the crumpled ball of bills into Renata's hands, then he was on the move again, down to the pasture where he took up the scythe and wildly swung at the grass.

"Looks like you have a new roommate, sweetheart." Mikhail heaved the Tracksuits into the back of van. Renata pulled the tarp from her Fiat and draped it over them.

"This isn't the end," Mikhail said.

Renata nodded.

"We'll watch the road, honey, but what's coming might be more than you can handle."

"Seems likely."

Mikhail handed her Maria's reins.

"You have some pears for her?"

...

Fattah had come out of the earth just north of the watering pond, not far from the old road that cut through the trees and ended at the river. Broken paving stones started at the edge of the woods, right next to an old wooden watch tower. At some point a bridge spanned the water: the pylons were still there. Renata assumed they'd dug under at this point, the shallowest the river was for some distance. On the other side, in Belarus, stood a few dilapidated service buildings. Nothing else.

"Ridiculous."

Fattah's escape hole had filled. Renata scooped up a handful, sipped then spitted. Spirit, she thought. 90%. Seemed like an incredibly stupid plan. Was there really money to be made this way? She considered Fattah. His black and blue face. What was one little Afghan to the Tracksuits? Were they even paying him? She still had doubts about letting them go. Maybe she could've gotten answers from them.

She turned back to the house. Fattah and Henryk followed.

They had a day, at least, maybe two. She first showed Fattah the Priest Hole and how to access it, doing her best to mime and explain that this was his hiding place when they came for him again, and how he could open the door from inside. He wasn't comfortable with guns—at least if how he held the semi-automatic Mauser was any indication—but she left it loaded down there for him, just in case. The Makarov she'd gotten off Tracksuits would stay in her front pouch pocket. She taped the Luger and a wooden block together on the underside of the kitchen table and sat in her chair to make sure she could unobtrusively reach for it to pull the trigger.

...

Three days after Mikhail drove the Tracksuits back across the border, he called.

"They're coming," he said. "You have five minutes at most."

She hung up and called the number, the one not written down. Anya had made her memorize it and repeat it back to her nearly every day. On the other end someone picked up but said nothing. Renata said what she had to say. The other end went to a dial tone before she hung up. She didn't know what to think of that. Seemed like a good idea, though, to disconnect the answering machine.

She opened the door to the Priest Hole and ushered Fattah to the opening, but he hesitated, began shaking his head and firing off words in Afghan.

"We don't have time for this," Renata said.

He looked back at her. Tears rivered down his cheeks. Was he afraid to go down, or was he worried for her?

"Ridiculous. Henryk, to me."

Though old, he was a smart dog, so perhaps he sensed the urgency in her voice. He scampered to her and didn't struggle when she plucked him up and shoved him into Fattah's arms.

"Now," she said.

After Henryk licked his face, Fattah nodded and backed carefully down the stairs. Renata clicked the bookcase shut.

She heard the car before she saw it. It was big. American. A Cadillac? Its driver was big too, even bigger than Mikhail. Well over two meters tall, and half as wide. Sunglasses. Long, dark trench coat. After parking in front of the barn, he hurried over to open the passenger door. A short, pudgy man dressed in white--from rounded hat to polished Oxfords--hopped out holding a phone. He shouted into it, punched it, and then shouted into it again. He pressed it to this ear and shook it. Cursing loudly in Russian, he pitched it out of Renata's view from the window; she heard it splash in the watering pond.

Who was that character? From that American serial about the two brothers? Boss Hogg. That's who this guy reminded her of.

She opened the door before they could knock. The driver said nothing, just reached down into the front pouch of Renata's coveralls, pulled out the Markarov and pocketed it. She raised her arms and slowly twirled, allowing a pat down. Apparently satisfied, he stepped aside.

"Thank you so much for accommodating my guard," Boss Hogg said, taking off his hat. "He insists on the precautions, though I don't anticipate any issues. Do you?"

Renata said nothing, simply turned and led them into the kitchen where she started the kettle. As expected the boss sat at the head of the table, with his back towards the wall. Renata prepared tea and a plate of biscuits. The guard's lumbering feet creaked across the floorboards in the bedroom. The chests opened and closed, as did the bathroom door. In the library he considered the guest bed, scanned the bookcases, peeked behind the curtains. The pictures and honors on the walls and on the desk made him stop. He bent over to look more closely, and then slowly pivoted his head towards the kitchen, peering over his sunglasses and squinting at Renata.

Boss Hogg took a small nibble of a chocolate-covered wafer. Apparently satisfied, he ate the rest of it and then gobbled down the remaining ones on the plate.

"Ah Polish hospitality," he said, before draining his tea. "But on to business. You know why I'm here, correct?"

Renata remained silent. She sat in the chair opposite him with hands in her lap. The Luger was inches away, still taped under the table. A quick belly shot. No problem. But the guard was another issue. Securing the gun with tape was, perhaps, not the best idea. Sure she could turn the gun, but, with the guard standing beside the boss, only his legs could be targeted; she could easily miss.

"You have some things of mine," Boss Hogg said. "I want them back."

Still she said not a word. He didn't seem to notice.

"Ah, I should've mentioned earlier. My boys. Not the brightest. Tweedle-Dee and Tweedle-Dum, I call them.

They don't know the allusion. Not big readers. They got their brains from their mother. Also their looks, God help them. But hey, they're family. What can you do? You spared them. I appreciate that. If killing you becomes necessary, I promise you it will be quick."

She didn't even flinch.

The guard bent down and whispered to his boss.

"Where's the woman?" Boss asked. "The one in the pictures?"

"Gone." And just as well, she thought. If she were still here, Dee and Dum would be dead, as would these two. Bullets between the eyes before their car even stopped. Oh, Anya, why did I let it get this far?

"Condolences. I'll assume she was your sister. Let's move on. Produce the van and our boy and we'll be on our way."

Silence still.

"As much as I've appreciated your hospitality, I'm a busy man. Honorable, too, though I have my limits. Your death will be quick. I promised you that. But what comes before, well..."

Far better people than her have lived far shorter lives. To be reunited with Anya. What kind of threat is death? But there was Fattah. Could she just leave him to his fate? She thought of the legend of the two skeletons found in the Priest Hole.

"Have you ever seen that film 'Alien?'" Boss Hogg said. "I love it. I even have a poster in my office. 'In space no one can hear you scream,' it says. Your place is so quiet, so secluded. Just one road in. Just like space."

Her right hand felt itchy. She rubbed her thumb against her trigger finger.

"Let's start with a finger," Boss Hog said.

"Uh, Boss, maybe we should..."

"Maybe? Maybe I shove a 3 iron up your ass. Do what you're told!"

The guard rolled his lips and stepped towards Renata. She lifted her right hand just enough to embrace the Luger. 744 days since I've seen you, she thought. Maybe that's long enough.

"So unnecessary," Boss Hog said. "I don't like blood. But business is business."

The guard thumbed open a switch blade. Renata lifted her right hand and embraced the Luger.

Renata looked up at the guard. A drop of sweat was ready to drip from his nose. The hand holding the knife. Was it shaking?

She pivoted her right hand, Luger still hidden but now aimed at his thigh. His eyes widened, then narrowed. He knew. The knife no longer shook. His free hand reached for her.

The phone rang. All three of them momentarily froze. The ring was jarring, louder than she'd ever heard it. Or at least it seemed that way. The guard waited for the boss.

"No answering machine?" Boss Hog asked. "Who doesn't have an answering machine?"

He nodded towards the library. The guard went, knife still open.

"Don't cut the cord. We might need it."

The guard lifted the receiver and immediately dropped it back onto the cradle.

"Now where were we?"

Or was it 745 days? The closing of the coffin. The earth opening its jaw. Why couldn't she remember? Since Fattah. The days have just blended together.

Before the guard made it back to the table, the phone started to ring once again.

"This is insufferable," Boss Hogg said. "You may answer your phone but one wrong word and I might have to rethink the whole 'quick death deal.'"

Renata remained seated. The phone continued to ring.

"Let's be reasonable. Answer the phone, and politely say you'll call back."

Renata shook her head. "It's for you."

"For me? She's a comedian, this one. A real Lucille Ball." He winked at his guard. "Go ahead and tell this very rude person who insists on interrupting my business that the lady of the house is indisposed."

The guard plodded back to the library, picked up the phone and listened. He took off the sunglasses and wiped his brow with a sleeve.

"Uh, Boss?"

"Now what? Need I remind you the 3 iron is in the trunk?"

"I think you should take this," the guard said.

Boss Hogg threw his hands up in the air. "Just goes to show that when you want a job done right..." He huffed and puffed to the library and tore the phone from his guard's hand.

"What!" he shouted into the receiver.

He said nothing more, just listened for some minutes, his free hand reaching up and smoothing back what hair remained on his head. Sweat had seeped into the pit of his suit jacket.

Renata reached under the table and peeled away the Luger. She could've easily plugged both goons then, but now there was no reason to.

She heard Anya: *Didn't I say I'd take always take care of you, little Mole?*

I'm sorry if I doubted you.

The tape had left some sticky stuff on the chamber. She picked at it with her thumbnail.

Boss Hogg carefully replaced the receiver back on the cradle. As his guard had done earlier, he did a doubletake when finally seeing the pictures on the wall. He opened his mouth and rubbed his jaw.

"You have, ah, some interesting friends," he said.

Renata blew on the Luger and wiped away the condensation with a napkin.

"You won't need that..."

"I know," Renata said.

The two men started to leave. Before they reached the front door, Renata called out:

"Afghanistan is far away. And plane tickets these days are pricy, or so I'm told. I've never actually been on a plane."

The two returned. Renata placed the Luger on the table.

"That place is a dump," Boss Hog said.

"So maybe his wife wants to leave," Renata said.

Boss Hogg nodded to his guard, who began fingering out German Marks. After stacking up a healthy pile of 100 Mark notes on the table, Boss Hogg raised his hand.

"He has two daughters," Renata said.

Boss Hogg sighed. His guard added more, and once the Marks were gone, he reached into another pocket for American Dollars and started a second pile.

"That's more than enough," Boss Hogg said.

"And three cats," Renata said.

"You're killing me. This is murder, pure and simple." Still, he flipped his fingers like he was brushing away a pesky fly. His guard dropped the rest of the hundred-dollar bills on the table.

"So much for one little digger," Boss Hogg said. "Please give me a chance to earn some of it back. This new economy isn't easy. I'll fix the tunnel, send in my bottlers. Set up in the woods. You'll never know they're here. We'll split the profits..."

"If that phone rings again you won't make it back across the border."

"Okay, okay." He plopped the hat back on his head and thumbed the brim. "There's always Lithuania."

He left then, cursing under his breath. His guard hesitated for a moment. Once his boss was through the front door, he turned and dipped into his pocket. Renata reached for the Luger. The man smiled, though.

"This might be useful." He placed a tattered Russian-Afghan dictionary on the table, and on top of that the Markarov. Bowing slightly he said, "My father had a Luger like that. Probably got his the same way as you."

She nodded and followed him outside. Up at the rise Mikhail sat on Maria. The Cadillac sped past and enveloped them with dust. Once it cleared Renata waved. Suddenly Fattah was at her elbow and Henryk at her heels.

"Such a sneaky little guy," she said.

There was so much to do now: first dinner, and then phone calls. Passports. Visas. They'd have to drain the pond and destroy the tunnel. And the clinic. Yes. Perhaps she should check in.

"Just a little longer," she said to the sky. "And then we'll have all of eternity."

PAST PERFECT

The classroom door crashed into a bookcase crammed with untouched sets of Jane Austin.

"Young man," a stranger in the doorway started. "Young man. I must speak. Please, yes? I must speak."

He had a hideous voice. The words rolled back and forth in a mouth overflowing with saliva, before something deep in his throat spat them out, each encased in a loud expulsion of breath. Every word was a struggle, as if his throat had been eaten away by cancer, or as if he were just learning to speak again after forty years of being mute.

"We must speak, now."

"As you can see," Frank said, "I'm in the middle of class. Come back later."

"Now, yes? We must speak now." This time, the words came out in a slow drawl, as if the stranger had imagined a comma between every word.

Frank sighed. A babble of Polish had erupted from the boys in back. The class was lost. Agata had been explaining the past perfect when the stranger interrupted. Frank excused himself. Agata, as usual, sat in the front row. Her head had dropped, and her hand grasped the silver crucifix she always wore on her necklace, the rush of blood turning her fingertips purple. Frank looked up. All the girls in the room had their eyes pinned to their desks. Most of the boys wore stupid grins.

"I'm fast, very fast," the man in the doorway said.

Some of the boys burst into laughter. Frank stared them into silence. He stepped out into the hallway, where the stranger offered him 200,000 Polish zlotys for a private English lesson, four times more than Frank ever charged.

"50,000, 100,000, 200,000," the man said. "These are only numbers. No jobs in America, no? I have CNN. Once Polish people go to America for to work. Now you go here. Very strange. But I have much money." He pulled a wad of zlotys from his pocket.

He had white, frizzled hair. The collar of his white button down was gray and there were cigarette burns in his blue polyester jacket. He hadn't yet shaved, even though it was almost noon, and his breath was a combination of smoke, home-doctored vodka and herring. And that voice, now that Frank had the opportunity to hear it up close, was made worse by the amplified popping of saliva bubbles and the discernible tapping of the tongue against tea-stained teeth. Frank's first impulse was to edge away from the man, feign an apology. But 200,000 zlotys. Almost sixteen dollars for an hour's easy work. After his contract expired in Poland, Frank wanted to swing a stop in Paris before moving on to his tour of Arthurian sites in England and Wales. A few hours a week with this guy and he might be able to leave untouched the stash he had made teaching in Qatar.

They made an appointment for that afternoon. They did not even bother to introduce themselves. Frank learned the stranger's name from a person whom he least expected it. During class, after he reentered the room, Frank asked if anyone knew the man who had so rudely interrupted Agata. Stefan, who had flat out refused to speak one word of English all year, stood up and said:

"That is Dr. Sempruch. He will win the Nobel Prize."

That set off a round of laughter Frank could only quell by excusing the class. But the laughter came only from the boys. The girls sunk deeper into their chairs.

...

Frank came to the uncomfortable realization that he had slept with every person in the teacher's room. Five women in the last six months, and only one spoke English. Frank paced around his desk and chain-smoked. He avoided eye contact with all of them. The women, however, were oblivious to his discomfort. They were well aware that they had passed him around, and Frank gathered, through his very limited Polish, that they had taken him on as some sort of charity case, that they had all read unhappiness and loneliness into his slumped profile, his downcast eyes and mouth, which seemed set into a permanent frown. To keep the American in Poland, they would make the "sacrifice." Frank's indiscretions had become a joke around the school. Even the Director contributed by saying, "A happy personal life means a happy professional life."

The doorknob rattled, then someone began pounding on the door. The five women continued to drink their tea and smoke their cigarettes. Frank stamped out his own, grabbed his coat and unlocked the door. To his relief, Dr. Sempruch was punctual.

"We hurry, yes," the Doctor said, as he began walking down the hall.

"Where are we going," Frank called after him. "You don't even know my name."

The Doctor turned around.

"You are Frank Mitchell, the American. Everybody know the American."

"You are just as famous, Dr. Sempruch."

"Everyone in Poland with much money are famous," the Doctor said.

The Doctor's Mercedes was parked on the road next to the viaduct that ran from the hill east of Kazimeirz Dolny, past the medieval town square, to the Vistula River. He deactivated the burglar alarm then opened the passenger's door for Frank.

The interior was all leather and smelled brand new. Dr. Sempruch eased behind the wheel and flipped open a false front under the dash, revealing a Blaupunkt CD player. He pressed a button and Frank was immediately assaulted, from six different speakers, by tinny, Polish electronic dance music.

"Where are we going?" Frank yelled.

The Doctor turned down the music.

"You don't like my car?"

"Of course. It's a nice car."

"I want the Cadillac," the Doctor said. He offered Frank a cigarette. They smoked quietly.

"Where's your office, Doctor?"

"Oh," he exclaimed, waving away Frank's question. He reached into the back seat and fumbled around. When he was settled back behind the wheel, he had a stack of magazines on his lap. The top one was *Playboy*. He flipped through the rest, all which looked brand new. Besides *Playboy*, he thumbed *Hustler*, *Penthouse*, *Screw*, *Gallery*, *Gent* and *Genesis*.

"What kind of Doctor are you, exactly?"

Dr. Sempruch didn't answer. He was busy removing the centerfolds from all the magazines. He unfolded the one from *Playboy* and held it up for Frank, and anybody else happening to pass by, to see.

"American girl," the Doctor said. "All American girls looks this way, yes?"

Unwittingly, Frank's eyes followed the unfolding of the woman. Her face was without blemish, her pale breasts high and firm, and her golden pubic hair allowed just a hint of her opening. Her turned to her blue, bottomless eyes and saw Agata there. The centerfold didn't even look like her. Agata probably had some Tartar in her, or at least Frank liked to think so; she had brown, "puppy dog" eyes, hair dark enough to appear black in the right light. Frank imagined her breasts to be larger, more round than the centerfold's. Nevertheless, he was looking at Agata.

The Doctor left out a raucous laugh and elbowed him in the arm. Frank must have been staring. He had even grown a little hard.

"Don't worry. I'm doctor. Good doctor. Much money." He kissed the centerfold, then placed it, along with the others, in the glove compartment.

"Yes," the Doctor continued, but in a serious tone, "all American girls looks like this. Or Joan Collins, yes? But you need Polish woman. The Polish woman cook, clean. But in America, only the Negro woman do this, yes?"

"We do understand one another," Frank said. "You do want English lessons?" He was trying to concentrate on business, but what he really wanted was to look through the damn magazines. He cracked open his window.

"Yes, yes," Dr. Sempruch said. "Everyone need English. He tossed all the magazines but the *Penthouse* into the back seat. He opened the magazine to the "Forum" section.

"For chrissakes," Frank said. "If you want to pay for lessons, fine, but enough of this crap."

Dr. Sempruch nodded.

"You are right," he said. "Very professional. Me, too."

But he kept the magazine in his lap. He placed his fingertip on the page and ran it slowly under the first line of the first "Forum" letter. It took him a while, giving Frank time to calm himself and light another cigarette. When the Doctor got to the fourth line he held the magazine under Frank's chin.

"This word," the Doctor said. "This word. 'Soont?'"

"Are you serious?"

"'Soont.'"

"This is the English lesson?"

"'Soont?'"

"Jesus. The word is 'cunt,' Doctor."

"Cunt," the Doctor said, then again, slowly: "C-u-n-t."

Doctor Sempruch again buried himself in the letter. Frank fidgeted with the door handle, opened the window a bit more, played with the stereo. He thought of Agata and her reaction, as well as the rest of the girls', to Dr. Sempruch. Who was this guy? Did he run around town showing his pecker to Frank's students? Frank could still picture Agata, the way she had held onto that crucifix.

"What's this?" the Doctor asked. "Lick 'poosy?' Lick 'poosy?' These English vowels."

"'Pussy,'" Frank said. "Lick pussy."

Doctor Sempruch raised his eyebrows.

"Lick pussy?" he asked. "Lick cat?"

"No, no," Frank said. "Lick pussy. To lick pussy. 'Pussy' is another word for 'cunt.' It's just a cunt."

"Oh," the Doctor said. "Ah, I understand!" He flipped the pages to a pictorial.

"Pussy! Cunt! Pussy! Cunt!" he exclaimed, jabbing at a vagina.

"Yes, yes," Frank shouted. "You got it."

"I understand!"

"You're one sick son of a bitch, you know that?"

"I now understand," the Doctor said. "You are good teacher."

They sat in the car for nearly an hour. After two of the letters, the Doctor was able to understand and correctly pronounce many of the American slang words for genitalia, all of which he wrote down phonetically in a pocket notebook. He was also exposed to new positions and techniques. These lessons, he maintained, were breaches in cultural barriers between Poland and the United States. He ended up giving Frank a 500,000 zloty note.

"You are good teacher," the Doctor said. "Number one. Better than others. Again next week, yes?"

"Why not," Frank said. "But next week maybe I'll bring a book?"

"Better than *Penthouse*?" the Doctor asked.

...

Many of his students had Frank over for dinner. Five months earlier, the Sunday after the American Thanksgiving, he ate with Agata's family for the first time. While Frank, Agata, her brother and mother ate roast pork and potatoes, her father, Mr. Rowinski, drank vodka. The man said only one sentence to Frank all evening: "You are from God's Country." This statement had followed his first half-liter bottle of vodka. Midway through his second, he slid to the floor and went to sleep.

Mrs. Rowinska took little notice of the lump on the floor. When serving dessert, she simply stepped over her husband. Midway through the cake, Agata burst into tears and ran into the kitchen. Her mother and brother became flustered only then, as if they were more shocked by Agata's behavior than of Mr. Rowinski's.

Despite the performance, Frank had been invited back once or twice a month since, so it was no surprise that on Friday, the day after Frank's first lesson with Dr. Sempruch, Agata knocked quietly on Frank's door.

"My mother would like you to come to us on Sunday,' she said. "For dinner."

As usual, her hair was tied back into a short ponytail. She wore a long woolen skirt and a loose sweater, which was anchored by that silver crucifix. She was so unlike many of the other sixteen-year girl students, with their incredibly tight leather skirts and their loose breasts bobbing behind nearly translucent blouses. Frank asked her to please come in--it was too cold to be without a jacket--but she refused, just repeated her rehearsed message in a stilted voice and left.

Frank turned back into his apartment and looked helplessly at the package sitting on his desk. He had been meaning to ask Agata to help him mail it out from the post office; he couldn't do it alone. She always helped him with such matters.

He picked up the package. This is the reason why I wanted her to come in, he thought, passing the package from one hand to the other. I need help with these things.

...

On Sunday, rain was falling, driving the drunks of Kazimierz to cover. Agata's apartment was only ten minutes by foot from Frank's, but he had to fight the cold wind and rain with his broken umbrella the entire way, so that by the time he reached his destination he was soaked through. Mrs. Rowinska ordered him to strip in the bathroom, sending him in with some of her husband's clothes. She spread Frank's wet clothes on the radiators scattered around the apartment. When Frank sat down in Mr. Rowinski's itchy trousers, he noticed, thankfully, that the table was set for four only. Was Mr. Rowinski drunk under a tree, he wondered, or "on business," that is, buying caviar in Lithuania to then sell in Belgium?

Mrs. Rowinska sat down only for the prayer, led by Agata. Both Mother and daughter were pious Catholics. Agata attended Mass twice a week and confessed every Saturday. She was also involved with youth groups organized by the priest and spent much of her spare time at the rectory, studying scripture and helping to groom the grounds.

During dinner, Mrs. Rowinska hovered around the table as Frank, Agata and Arek, Agata's younger brother, ate in silence. They had just begun the main course when Frank said: "Doctor Sempruch is a weird guy."

"Weird," Agata said. "What is 'weird?'"

"Well, he's a boobie," Frank said.

"He go to boobie-hatch!" Arek squealed.

"I don't know this," Agata said, poking at the chicken on her plate.

Agata's hair hung loosely on her shoulders, framing her long white neck. She gazed at her food.

"Boobie or not," Frank said. "He's a rich Pole and I'm a poor American. I'm tutoring him."

"Poor American!" Arek shouted.

After a long moment, Agata shrugged and pushed her full plate away.

...

After dessert, the rain still falling, they played some of the card games Frank had taught them on earlier visits. Rummy "500" was Mrs. Rowinska's favorite. She didn't win, but her kids made her laugh till she almost cried, and between hands, she kept up a steady supply of cake and tea from the kitchen, even though Arek repeatedly rummied her and looked at the cards she left face down on the table. For once Mrs. Rowinska, with wet cheeks and wide smile, looked the thirty-five she was, not the slumped over fifty-year old Frank sometimes ran into at the market or on the square. Her husband was out there somewhere, beyond the blurred window, the patter of the rain drowning out his footsteps, wherever they were leading.

After a supper of sliced sausage, cheese and fresh rolls, Frank sunk into the couch with his cigarettes. Arek leaned into him, his head on Frank's shoulder, laughing at "Winnie the Pooh" on television. Frank laughed as well, even though he didn't understand most of the dialogue. As television shows rolled by, Mrs. Rowinska showed Frank photographs of the Warsaw that existed before the Nazis demolished it.

Agata was at the table, studying a picture she was drawing of Sir Gawain, Frank's favorite among all the Arthurian knights. The rain continued uninterrupted, the glow from the television filled the darkening room with a blue mist. By nine, Arek was asleep on his shoulder. Frank had no wish to disturb the scene. He felt more at home here than he did in the cavernous apartment the director of the school let him use, more comfortable than he ever felt, in the last months of his marriage, in his own apartment in Cincinnati. But he slid away from Arek, who just moaned and continued his sleep. Both Mrs. Rowinska and Agata showed him to the door. He quickly put on his overcoat and slipped his hands into the pockets. In the right one, he found an envelope that was not there when he left home. He began to pull it out. Agata grabbed his wrist tightly.

"Please," she said quietly, but with force. "I will see you at the school."

Quickly, an image of her naked popped into Frank's mind: white skin, full breasts, just a small triangle of pubic hair. He pulled his arm away and held his rolling stomach. He did not know where the image came from, or how such a thing could so quickly replace the feeling of family love he had been experiencing all night.

He lurched through the door. Not until he was out in the pouring rain, the five-hundred year-old square of Kazimierz a blur in front of him, did Frank realize that he was still in Mr. Rowinski's clothes.

...

The following week, Agata did not come to school. Frank only had her for two classes a week to begin with. He asked the other teachers about her. No one seemed to know why she was absent or when she would return. On Tuesday, after the class Agata normally attended, Frank folded her father's clothes and delivered them to her apartment. After

Mrs. Rowinska repeated herself a few times, Frank was able to figure out that Agata wasn't at home, that she was at the rectory. Why doesn't she come to school? he attempted to ask. Mrs. Rowinska just squinted and invited Frank over for dinner on Sunday.

The letter remained in Frank's jacket. He was convinced, whether out of guilt or self-pity, that Agata was somehow instigating the sexual fantasies he was stricken with. What she had so secretly delivered to him must be a "love" letter, the type students pass to one another when they think Frank's not paying attention. Over the years he had received dozens of them. From his stint as a high school teacher, to his days as a teaching assistant at the University of Cincinnati, even in Qatar. Would he, could he answer this one? He was leaving Poland in two months. He would never be back. And even if caught, nothing would happen to him. Christ, the summer before the gym teacher had impregnated two students. The girls were punished for "bad behavior." The gym teacher didn't even get a slap on the wrist.

On Thursday, when Agata failed to appear, Frank gave the class a writing assignment and rushed to the teacher's room, where his coat hung. He snapped. He had to see the letter. After four days of discipline he was so anxious that it took him a few minutes to get the damn key to the door to work. He finally swung the door open. The other teachers were smoking their cigarettes and drinking their tea. They ignored Frank. Even Beata, who he had just slept with, paid him no heed. He grabbed his coat. In the hall, after a moment's hesitation, he took the letter from the pocket. The envelope was addressed to Dr. Sempruch.

Frank was so disappointed that he never even thought about what the letter might contain, what business such a sweet innocent like Agata could have with a loathsome creature like Dr. Sempruch. He even went so far to convince himself that the letter was one of those teenager ploys: "Let Frank know that I like him, but don't tell him I said so. Just say that you *know*. Write me back and describe his reaction."

Later that afternoon, Frank sat in Dr. Sempruch's Mercedes. The car was parked in the same place it had been the week before. Frank suggested they go somewhere else for the lesson, like to the Doctor's place, or to Frank's. Dr. Sempruch waved the suggestion away and adjusted his seat. Frank sighed. He lit a cigarette and opened the anthology of short stories he had brought along. After five minutes though, the Doctor had grown bored with the Hemingway story and suggested they look at an old *Penthouse*.

Frank feigned defeat. He could barely concentrate. His sexual fantasies about Agata were coming in a flurry, and as their intensity increased, Frank's curiosity about the letter's content became obsession. While the doctor poured over a pictorial, Frank fingered the letter in his pocket.

"You are very famous, Doctor," he said. "At least among my students."

"Many patients."

Frank took out the letter and dropped it into the Doctor's lap, covering Miss December's attributes.

"From a student," Frank said tentatively. "Agata Rowinska? Is she a patient, or maybe her mother?"

Doctor Sempruch shrugged. He tore open the envelope and read the page long note slowly, his finger moving under the lines, as it had with the "Forum" letters.

Frank tried to appear disinterested. He flipped through the anthology, even slid the *Penthouse* off the Doctor's lap to have a closer look. After nearly five minutes, his finger three-fourths down the page, the Doctor turned to Frank and snickered.

"What does it say?"

The Doctor again shrugged. He finished the letter and, to Frank's confusion, started the car.

"We go to my office," Dr. Sempruch said.

The Doctor's office was just a few miles from Kazimierz, in the hamlet of Bochotnica, a web of dirt roads and tiny farms that spun off the Warsaw highway. In front of a boxy two-story house, the Mercedes slid to a stop, drawing a tired stare from a dirty ewe grazing in the side yard and scattering a group of skinny chickens that had been lightly treading the gravel.

"This is where you work?" Frank asked. There was no sign proclaiming the Doctor's occupation affixed next to the front door. Like all the other houses in the hamlet, the Doctor's was built of cinderblocks, and looked as if it would always be in a perpetual state of incompletion; a concrete balcony jutted out of the second floor, right above the front door, yet it had no railing and because some of the concrete had fallen, the rusty iron rods holding it up were visible. The upstairs windows were still spotted with the dull yellow paint that had done little to relieve the drabness of the thin layer of stucco covering the cinderblocks. The rain gutter meant for the front of the house lay on the side of the driveway. The chickens pecked water from it.

"Good place for me," the Doctor said. "Close to Warsaw, but not so close, yes?" He unlocked the dead bolt and ushered Frank into the house.

...

"What are you talking about?" Frank asked. He and the Doctor were sitting on a big, soft couch that could have come straight from the Sears' catalog. The Doctor seemed to own none of the types of furniture usually found in Polish houses: hard, uncomfortable couches and chairs that invariably opened into equally uncomfortable beds, or into storage chests. But like most other Polish homes, Frank thought, the Doctor's was impeccably clean. The stooped over old woman with bad teeth who served them cakes was probably the caretaker, but Dr. Sempruch ignored her completely, so Frank didn't ask.

"You are good teacher," the Doctor said. "I take care of you. No pain. Snip, snip. Suck, suck. Over and done."

"I'm lost here," Frank said.

"No money even," the Doctor said. "A 'freebie,' you call this?"

"There's nothing the matter with me," Frank said. "What the hell is in that letter?"

"With you," the Doctor said. "No, you are full man!" He slapped Frank on the knee and pulled himself out of the sofa.

"Just tell me what the hell is going on here."

The Doctor laughed. From behind the couch he took a medical instrument that to Frank looked like large barbecue tongs. He clicked it open and closed in front of Frank's nose.

"I'm very good," the Doctor said. "Careful, can I say?"

"Just what does that letter say?"

"Oh," the Doctor said. "It don't matter. You're business. I keep secrets good."

"Gimme that goddamn letter!" Frank lunged for the Doctor. He first hit the coffee table, which balanced on two legs for a brief moment before crashing onto its face, throwing cakes, cups of tea and a large vase onto the inlaid, wooden floor. Frank shoved the Doctor down into the shattered glass and pottery.

"I said, give me that letter."

Dr. Sempruch remained on the floor. He lifted the letter from under a small pile of broken glass, wiped off the puddle of tea and held it out. Frank was calm again. He wanted to rip the letter from the Doctor's hand in one more show of anger, but then just mumbled "Sorry" and took the envelope with his shaking hand.

Of course Frank couldn't read the Polish. Yet he still went through each line. He was afraid to look at the Doctor. He kept the letter until his hands stopped shaking. His name appeared three different times.

"My name is here," he said. "Why is my name here?"

"Why?" the Doctor replied. "Why?"

The old woman started cleaning up the mess. The Doctor was still on the floor.

"My name is in this letter, Doctor. Why is my name here?"

"But you know this girl," the Doctor said. "Yes?"

"She's my student. She's sixteen."

"Ah, sixteen," the Doctor said, sighing. "Not so young."

"What does that mean? She's a student. A young student. Tell me what the letter says."

With slow deliberation, the Doctor got up from the floor, brushing off his pants and sleeves. To Frank, he took on an aura of aloofness; he kept his chin high, moved with more thought, as if he were realizing a new power over the American. Even his voice seemed less raspy.

"I will show my office," he said. "Very clean. The girl is worrying too much. I'm good doctor."

"Your office? With chickens and sheep running around?"

"You also worry. Is very clean here."

The Doctor opened the door leading into an adjoining room. There was a table, stirrups, polished instruments. The walls were stark white and contained no windows.

"My girls," the Doctor said. He nudged Frank in the ribs and pointed to the ceiling. It was covered with centerfolds. Months and months of blondes, brunettes, redheads. Some were in conservative poses, showing only a breast, or a view of their behind. Others had their legs spread wide and opened their vaginas with finely sculpted fingers. This would be the view for anyone splayed out on the table.

"What kind of Doctor are you?" Frank asked, aghast, yet mesmerized by this collage of perfect breasts and perfect faces.

"The patient say you worry. Maybe you, Frank Mitchell, don't want this abortion?" The Doctor glanced at the letter in Frank's hand.

"What? Me? Why should I..." He followed the Doctor's eyes.

"Jesus. The letter names me the father?"

...

Midway through that first sleepless night after his visit to the Doctor's, Frank lay in bed with his dog-eared copy of

Chretien de Troyes' *Arthurian Romances*. From his window he saw a corner of the medieval square. A nearly full moon blazed away in the cloudless sky, and its rays reflected off the bleached white, ruined castle and the wide river, illuminating the hillside Kazimierz perched upon with a dull, ghostly glow. Frank wasn't melodramatic enough to launch himself into this perfect medieval setting, to become the knight on the white charger and avenge the wrong done to Princess Agata. Yet he thought of the world of King Arthur, where a moment's hesitation towards a lady could lead to a lifetime of scorn, or even a fleeting thought of adultery was reason enough to have your head lopped off. Frank was beginning to wonder if this strange episode in his life, this ridiculous letter, was to be retribution for a past injustice towards a woman, whoever, wherever, she was. Maybe he screwed somebody over, fathered a child, moved on without leaving an address. Like a knight-errant, he would have to make up for past digressions, whether or not present and past had any clear connections.

So insane, he said to himself, over and over. But how else could he justify Agata's slander? Or his desire to help her? He could not say that he and Agata were "close." Like the last visit, he had spent many pleasant Sundays with her family. Agata helped him overcome language and cultural barriers, had shown him historical monuments all over the area, and had made sure he wasn't alone on the holidays. She was his liaison. In turn, Frank had made little effort to get to know her. He wondered now if his sexual fantasies were not but a defense mechanism to stop genuine feelings for her. He would be leaving Poland soon. Like many other acquaintances left scattered in his mobile past, his and

Agata's would soon be left to the occasional letter and Christmas card. Whether Frank liked it or not, Agata had broken down his defense, had forced his hand. Her specific intentions in implicating him as the father were, of course, unclear. First things first. He wanted to know who violated her, who transformed her from a sweet maiden to another appointment for Dr. Sempruch.

Agata made the first move. When Frank looked out his window Saturday morning, he saw a yellow note taped to the glass. All it said was, "15:00. Castle tower." Frank recognized the handwriting. At a quarter to three he dressed quickly. After a moment's thought, he grabbed the yet unmailed package.

Outside, all signs of the cold, rainy weather that had plagued early spring were gone. The countryside was beginning to bloom. The cobblestoned streets of Kazimierz were alive with flower peddlers, Russian traders, and German tourists snapping pictures of their children who leaned against the lonely wooden well that rose up in the middle of the square. The cafes had spread out onto the patios covered by gabled, wooden roofs, and their tables were filled with daytripping Varsovians and ragged artists who put their sketches down long enough to nurse a beer or espresso, and to strike up conversations with Scandinavian backpackers.

Package in hand, Frank worked his way through the bustling activity of the square and up along the staircase arrangement of the Parish church, cemetery, castle ruins, and at the top, the isolated castle tower. At the tower Frank looked back and watched birds circle the hodge-podge of houses and their orange roofs that descended toward the river.

As if in hiding, Agata suddenly appeared from the alcove of trees to one side of the tower.

Frank stepped toward her and said quickly, "I have this package to mail. It's one of those chess sets I got in Cracow. Well, you were with me, weren't you. Remember?"

"Today is Saturday," she said in a calm, soft voice. "The post office is closed."

"Yeah, right. I know. But Monday, maybe?"

Agata didn't answer. She took a few steps to her left. Frank immediately fell into step with her, as if he knew where they were going and why. They slid down a short, steep incline onto a well-trodden path. The forest path linking Kazimierz to the castle ruins above Bochotnica.

"Soon you are away from Poland," Agata said, breaking their silence. "What do you do then?"

The first stage of the path was hard as cement, despite the recent rain. The trees to the sides met above them in an arched canopy. They could have been walking down the aisle of a Gothic cathedral. They passed backpackers on the path. That's all. On this picture-perfect day, Frank expected lovers around every bend.

"What *will* I do once I leave Poland?" Frank corrected. He told her of his plans to tour "Arthur's Britain," writing articles along the way. Then he intended on continuing his Phd studies at the University of Cincinnati.

He was too easily led astray from the subject on his mind. No wonder, since he didn't really want a confrontation with Agata. Frank remembered a rape case somewhere in the Carolinas. A man was found guilty of the crime. Eight or so years later, the "victim" confessed that the man languishing in jail was completely innocent. The woman had made up the entire story. Frank tried to speculate what would happen if the two met on the street someday. What would the man say or do? Would he try to kill her? Would he forgive her? Would he simply walk away without saying a word?

As Agata made small talk, Frank stared at her. She was dressed conservatively, as usual. She still wore the silver crucifix and more often than not she held it. Frank had expected her to look different. Somehow. On the surface, she remained the sweet Agata Frank had known.

"Who did it?" he blurted out.

Agata paused, then continued talking about the weather and summer holidays.

"Who did it?" he repeated, in a voice he usually reserved for disobedient students.

"It is no matter," she said.

"No matter?" Frank said. "No matter?"

"The other question you have is easier," she said.

"Question? I have only one question," he said, lighting a cigarette. He stopped and put his hand on Agata's shoulder.

"Who's the *real* father?"

She turned towards Frank, the crucifix gripped in her small hand. Behind her, in a clearing stood what was left of the Bochotnica castle; just two walls, one, with three holes, looking to Frank like a Dramatist's mask, but instead of a happy or sad face, the impression given off by the large, round hole blown open by a Swedish cannon was one of astonishment.

"You," Agata said.

"Me?" Frank said, spinning away from her. "Me? This is insane. I'm going insane. Agata, listen to me. I'm not the father. I'm your teacher, for chrissakes. You're sixteen. I'm thirty-seven. Do you understand? I'm old enough to be your father. I could be *your* father."

Oh, God, Frank thought. I'm making her cry.

But Agata didn't cry. She didn't move. She looked up at Frank as if totally bewildered. Her eyes were wide and glassy, her lips slightly parted. One hand hung limp at her side, the other, surrounding the crucifix, shook and turned darker with blood as Frank watched.

"Okay," Frank said. "Okay, Agata. This is it. We can go home, or we can go to the Doctor's. Either way, I'm with you. Okay? Just let go of your necklace. You're hurting yourself."

With the ruins behind her, the trees around her, and no sounds but the rustling of the new leaves and an occasional birdcall, Agata looked like a little child lost. She bit into her lip.

"Let go of that thing," Frank said, prying her fingers from the crucifix. She relaxed her fingers. The crucifix fell to the ground. It was covered with blood.

"Jesus Christ," Frank said.

Agata shook her head again, then suddenly stopped and looked down at the crucifix.

Her father did it, Frank realized. That fucking drunk did it. Of course. No, of course not. How could a father do that to his own kid? Impossible. No, not impossible. The gym teacher could do it, a priest could do it. I could do it. Any man could do it. In America, in Poland. Anywhere. I don't know what a father could do. I'm not a father. I only know what a man could do.

"Goddamn him," Frank said.

"Don't say this," Agata said. Now she started to cry.

"Goddamn that son of a bitch," Frank said.

"Please, don't say this," Agata said.

"He's a goddamn bastard."

"Please," she said.

Frank took her into his arms.

"The letter, there is no choice," she said.

"It's okay, it's okay," Frank said. He held her. She sobbed into his chest. This was the first time he had felt her body pressed to his. His desire was to comfort this child.

She wants me to be a father? Frank thought. I can do that. I can marry her mother, take the whole family away from this place. This I can do. But first things first. Get rid of the monster in her. Then everything will be clear. Everything will be better.

Frank eased Agata from his arms and took her hand. In front, above, on either side, rose the cathedral of trees. Beyond, at the end of the path, Dr. Sempruch's office. Frank picked up the bloodied crucifix and dropped it into his pocket. Hand in hand, the couple descended down the path.

"Just promise me you'll keep your eyes closed," Frank said. "Promise me."

THE SILENT FALL

On the fifteenth day of his son's silence, Tadeusz was shaken awake by shotgun blasts reverberating through the forest of Stalinist blocks. He arose hoping that the drunkard Yeltsin had gone insane and launched an invasion of Poland. But no, the thunder echoing between the blocks was not bullets pockmarking the stucco, or artillery shells blowing apart his neighbors, but Mrs. Konwicka pounding her rugs into submission in the courtyard. Tadeusz studied his rumpled self. He had slept in his clothes again, and the cheap plum wine he had been drinking the night before stained his warm-up suit. He swung open the window and let the cool autumn breeze flow in, anything to dispel the musty smell now permeating the main room of the flat.

Tadeusz turned back to the room and looked down at his son. The boy stared straight into his bulging stomach. He was dressed in his First Communion clothes: a navy-blue suit, an old silk tie his mother had cut and sewn into an appropriate size, white socks and a pair of summer sandals.

"What's this, little man?" Tadeusz asked.

To no surprise, the boy remained silent.

Right, Tadeusz thought. Sunday. He kicked aside the piles of his clothes and stood in front of the bedroom door.

"Hey," he shouted. "Our boy's ready for Mass!"

He rattled the knob and swung open the door. He half expected his wife to be in another man's arms, but the room was empty, the bed pushed back into a couch.

"Where's your mother, little man?"

The boy hadn't moved since Tadeusz awoke.

"Did she at least feed you?" he asked. "If not, I can prepare something. What do you want? You name it."

When the boy still refused to speak, Tadeusz fought the inclination to grab him by the shoulders and shake him. His dear boy. He knelt in front of him and placed his hands on the boy's cheeks.

"How about eggs. Just you and me. After, we can go kick around the ball. How about that?"

The front door flew open, and Tadeusz's wife, dressed in the smock she wore to work at the fruit and vegetable stand, charged up to Tadeusz and grabbed his wrists.

"Keep your hands off him," she said. "Come here, Mateusz." She pulled the child into her arms and brushed the back of his head with her open hand.

"Mateusz and I are going to the park to kick around the ball," Tadeusz said. "How about some breakfast?"

"He ate an hour ago," she replied. "And you know where the kitchen is."

Tadeusz slumped into his unmade bed and lit a cigarette.

"Daddy's going to take you to church this week, okay Sweetheart?" she said.

"The hell, I am. We're playing football."

"Yes, you are," she said. "I have to open the shop today. And when you get back you will clean up this mess."

"You say that like a wife."

"I don't need to be reminded of that."

If I were less of a man, I'd slap that stupid scowl off her face, Tadeusz thought. The harlot.

While she fussed with the boy, Tadeusz wedged into the tiny bathroom and examined his face. He didn't remember shaving yesterday, but apparently he had. The bruises on his cheeks and around his left eye had turned a disgusting yellow. The one front tooth that had been knocked loose was beginning to tighten, but he still didn't dare brush. Instead, he rubbed his teeth with toothpaste, forcing his finger to the back rows until he gagged and almost threw up what little remained in his stomach. Before leaving the bathroom and confronting his wife, he again looked at his face and wondered how many years he had left before the girls lost interest in him.

His wife had laid out a new, clean white shirt on his bed.

"You do love me after all," he said, infusing his voice with that flirtatiousness she had once loved long ago.

"Right," she said. "Your mother left that and took a pile of your clothes home to wash. If you had any love at all for the old woman you'd wash your own damn clothes."

"How about a kiss," he said.

"Maybe in the next life," she said.

...

The church was a dilapidated old warehouse, with a tin roof that leaked and folding chairs instead of pews. The rector of the parish had been promising the new church would be ready soon, for three years. Instead of building the church on schedule, he erected the parish house first, a gaudy red brick affair with a red roof and numerous gables. The men in the parish nicknamed it "Malbork," after the Teutonic castle near Gdansk. Tadeusz hated the rector and begrudged every zloty his wife dumped into the man's till. He hadn't attended Mass in months, and the old birds in their lace-swathed dresses, who ignored the rector's money grubbing and philandering, let him know it with whisperings and stares. He tried to steer his boy to a back row, but Mateusz kept walking up the center aisle, would have sat next to the altar for all Tadeusz knew, if he hadn't finally shoved the kid into a cluster of chairs behind the rector's niece, a fat woman who offered shelter from the eyes of her uncle.

During the mass, Mateusz sang every hymn, repeated every prayer, and read along with each excerpt from the bible. Tadeusz stared at him in amazement. Who was this kid, he wondered, and how long has he been going on like this? He didn't want his one child to turn into some freak. It's bad enough he showed little interest in football or basketball. What struck him even more than the kid's piety, though, was his voice. It was the first time he'd heard it in two weeks. He bent closer just to savor the words. If only all these other fools would quit their muttering.

Mateusz fell into enraptured silence for the sermon. You'd think the Pope himself was speaking about the easiest way to get to heaven, not the damn rector demanding more and more money for the building of the new church. Tadeusz drifted off and revisited his first time with Kasia.

He had been eyeing her all year, the coquette, with her tight little skirt and perky breasts. She cut class on a regular basis, and sometimes she'd sashay past the football pitch on her way to the back of the building for a smoke. Tadeusz's eyes would follow her until his boys took note of his mental absence and reduced their game to a screaming brawl. When the weather began to turn and his physical fitness classes started basketball and calisthenics in the gym, he sought her out at the end of the day and scolded her for her poor performance in school.

"What do I care," she told him. "I have a rich lover in Switzerland who will take care of me."

"How old is he?"

"Oh, he's old," she said, revealing that row of teeth made perfect by an uncle reaping a fortune in Geneva.

She left him then, eyeing him over her shoulder, as he fingered a few well-worn zlotys in his pocket.

In February, at the party celebrating the beginning of the last one hundred days of the school term, Tadeusz, wobbly on too much vodka and Georgian champagne, followed her down a darkened hallway.

"I used to be a star," he drawled, the alcohol once again bringing up this old story he had told so many times before. It had worked once on the girls, years ago, but what did this new generation care about the Olympics, and football and Soviet boycotts? He was too drunk, however, to notice that the laughter in Kasia's throat was mocking jest, not revelry.

"A Striker! That's what I was. I wound my way around the toughest defenses and always found my mark."

"Ooh, I bet you did, Professor Styś."

"Damn right. I should wear medals! All I got is an ugly wife."

"She's beautiful," Kasia said.

Now, the party, which took place in the other wing of the school, was but a dull roar.

"She's old," Tadeusz said. "You're beautiful."

He pulled her into a recess and bent to kiss her. She turned her head, and while he pecked at her cheek like a hungry chicken she whistled a tune.

"I always find my mark." He reached under her skirt and cupped her ass.

"Professor Styś, what would the director say?"

"That old bastard? If he could find his dick beneath all that fat he'd fuck you, too." Still stabbing at her cheek, he wedged a hand between her legs. She spun away from him, so easily that he just stood there amazed and stared at the finger that had come so close.

"Maybe next time," she called over her shoulder. Her heels tapped the hallway and she retreated back to the party, whistling the same tune the whole way.

Tadeusz was still young enough to think that there is always a next time, at least as far as girls were concerned. Life is full of second chances just waiting to pop out at you like a beast in a forest. Right before the last hour one day in mid-June, Tadeusz handed a basket to his target and told her that she must go to his garden and pick the strawberries he was sure were peaking. She rolled her eyes but took the basket. Such a request from a teacher wasn't an unusual one. Besides, Tadeusz hadn't bothered her all spring. There was no reason for her to expect funny business.

Tadeusz let his last class go early and ran ahead to his garden home. When Kasia arrived, swinging the basket, he was waiting for her. He downed a shot of vodka and poked his head out, around the plastic sheet serving as a window to the small shack at the far end of his garden plot.

"Strawberries indeed," she called out.

"It's a little early. How was I supposed to know?" he said.

When she turned to go, Tadeusz hurried to the door and opened it.

"How about a smoke?" he asked.

"Sure," she said. "Bring it over."

"The Director's plot is over there," he said. "He usually comes poking around about now. You better come in."

She dumped the basket and followed him inside.

Easier than I imagined, he thought. The little slut.

He lit the cigarette for her and placed it between her thin lips. She raised her left eyebrow.

"Well?" she asked.

...

Later on, after her pregnancy became known, she would tell the Director, as well as her father, that she never expected Professor Styś to go so far. How could she? She was only seventeen. A teacher might play around a bit, but there were limits, weren't there?

Tadeusz noticed his son standing, waiting to get by him. The sermon had finally ended. He crossed his legs and shifted to his side to let the boy pass. He just stood there.

"Go on," Tadeusz said.

Mateusz remained. His father realized that he was expected to take communion as well.

"I haven't been to confession," he whispered. When the boy still didn't move, Tadeusz sighed and made his way to the aisle. The boy even reached for his hand. When Tadeusz felt the warmth in his palm a wave of guilt struck him full and almost made him double over in pain. It passed quickly, however, and as they waited in line, Tadeusz whispered to his son that he'd be waiting outside. He pulled his hand away and walked quickly towards the door. When he got to the end of the aisle, he turned and instinctively knelt.

Mateusz was watching him. Tadeusz crossed himself. Only then did his boy look back to the altar.

Some of his old pals were on the steps smoking and laughing quietly. Tadeusz still had a few flattened cigarettes in his pocket, but they were Russian and tasted like the smoke from burning tires. Leszek was there though, a soft touch who had started up a recycling business on European Union funds and drove a brand-new Volvo.

"How about a Camel?" Tadeusz asked him.

"You threw up in my car and didn't even clean it up," Leszek said.

"Come on, Lesz," Tadeusz said. "You know how it's been."

Indeed he did. The whole fucking town knew about Kasia ratting on Tadeusz. The kids of these men standing next to him went to the same school and knew that Tadeusz's responsibilities had been cut in half this year, a good sign that he wouldn't be around at all next year. What's happening to this country? Tadeusz wondered. A man makes a mistake now and he's shoved out like week-old bread.

Tadeusz stuffed his hands in his pockets and shook his head. Leszek heaved a sigh and held out his cigarette pack.

Tadeusz lit up. Now that he was part of the group again he relaxed and started in on his old tirade.

"It's that bastard, Wałesa," he said. "He's got a bishop as a right-hand man now? Just wait and see. We'll have our own Inquisition right here. You got these sons of whores in the kiosks poking holes in condoms with pins. What's next?"

"No more divorce?" Marek said.

"That's right," Tadeusz said, pointing at him with his cigarette.

"Mandatory church?" Michal said.

"You've got it."

"They start taking the Tithe right out of our pay?"

"It's coming," Tadeusz said, squeezing his hand into a fist. The guys were laughing now, though, and Tadeusz blushed. They all used to be inseparable, back in the old days. At least when the Communists were around you knew who your friends were.

The guys started drifting away, meeting up with their wives and children who streamed out of church. Tadeusz waited and waited for Mateusz. Even the old birds beat him out. Tadeusz walked up the stairs and peered inside. Sure enough the kid was kneeling at the altar. Tadeusz, his worn sneakers aiding him, snuck up on the boy and listened to him murmur some prayers before he grabbed his shoulders and yelled "Surprise!"

"Don't worry," he said, rubbing his son's shoulders. "It's only me, not Jesus."

Mateusz crossed himself.

"What are you praying for, son? Your mother and I will fix things. We've been through worse."

Mateusz looked straight ahead.

"Jesus had the right idea. He never married," Tadeusz said and chuckled.

Mateusz crossed himself again and stood.

"Now we can play football," Tadeusz said.

...

The wind had picked up. Tadeusz tasted the promise of snow and ice, yearned for the slight anonymity the Polish winter would afford him. Too many people will be too busy struggling with their scarves to point to him on the street;

others, hurrying from warm house to warm store, back to warm house, will be too self-absorbed in fuel bills to whisper when he walks by. Then he could wander the streets in peace.

He dribbled the ball, his eyes moving from his son who stared at the ground, to the bare goal Tadeusz defended.

"Okay, little man. Let's see what you've got." He rolled the ball to Mateusz. "Remember what I told you. Keep your back straight, bend the knees."

Tadeusz crouched in position.

"Fire!"

Mateusz did not kick the ball.

"I'm waiting."

Tadeusz waited for two minutes, bobbing back and forth on his feet, his arms outstretched like a wrestler. Mateusz just stood there with his hands in his pockets.

"I know you're cold, little man. One or two solid hits will warm you up. Trust me just this once. Can you do that for your father?"

Mateusz didn't move.

"Okay, then. Do it for your mother. You know how much she'd love to see you score on me?"

Mateusz took his eyes from the ground and gazed into the distance, towards the general vicinity of his home.

"That's it," Tadeusz said. "She'd love it." He averted his eyes as well. Something else took away his attention, too; maybe a bird, or a falling leaf, or a passing girl defying the change in weather with an impossibly short skirt. Whatever it was, his momentary distraction was quickly followed by the football slamming into his nose. He didn't feel it on impact, just the quick rush of breath forcing itself out of his body when his back landed on the hard ground.

Time and space slipped by. There was no pain then, just sweet silence and a becoming darkness that danced before his eyes. So this is the way it was for his father in the last months before Alzheimer's took him away for good. Not until the blood seeped between his lips did he realize what had happened. The pain hit him when he raised his head to first scold, and then to congratulate his boy, his darling boy who had some fire in him after all.

There was no sight of Mateusz, however. His father bleeds all over God's creation, and the boy just walks away. No matter, Tadeusz thought. The kid's a champ.

...

"Kasia's father beat you up again?" his wife asked later that evening.

"Very funny," Tadeusz said. "Besides, he caught me when I wasn't looking. I didn't know he was insane. Ask anyone who was there. Ask the boy.

"No," Taduesz continued. "This is the work of my son. His father's son! Tell her, Mateusz. Tell her how your ferocious kick put your old man flat on his back. Go ahead."

Mateusz had been absorbed with "Winnie-the-Pooh" on the television when Tadeusz came home. The show ended then, but instead of bragging to his mother, Mateusz switched off the television and took up his mathematics workbook.

"Let me check your homework, honey," his mother said.

"What the hell does the kid need math for, or religion, for that matter," Tadeusz said. "He's going to be a pro. He's going to leave this god-forsaken country and get rich playing for Manchester United. Just you watch, with the proper training..."

Seeing that no dinner was coming his way, Tadeusz took a bus to his mother's flat across town. He retold the story of his son's athletic prowess while she changed the dressing on his nose. Both his eyes were black again, and the swelling in his face made it difficult to talk.

"It's time he starts a rigorous training program," Tadeusz said. "I hope it's not too late. I should have recognized it sooner. The Brazilians can dribble before they walk."

"Is he talking to you yet?" his mother asked.

"Any day now," Tadeusz said. "Any day now."

...

Little sleep was to be had that night. Every time Tadeusz tried to roll over on his side, burying his face into the pillow, searing pain surged into his head. When he did find sleep, the same dream kept replaying in his mind's eye: his father, weeks before he died, kept trying to leave the apartment in his underwear in the middle of the night.

"Where are you going?" Tadeusz asked in the dream.

"Somewhere else," his father always said.

Tadeusz pulled himself out of bed and went to the window to watch the sun rise. In his last months, Tadeusz's father sat in a chair and stared into space. As his death loomed closer, he recognized his wife and son less and less often. His father was once a powerful man, who, with his booming voice, corralled his employees at the bank, as well as his wife and children, into quiet obedience. But at the end, he sat as still as a well-fed kitten. His wife fed him, bathed him, paid the bills. Even alive he was no longer part of this world. Not even a hunger for sex gnawed at his gut. Lucky bastard.

Out of the corner of his eye, Tadeusz noticed the unmistakable shape of his wife's purse in the shrinking shadows of the kitchen. He dressed quickly, pulling back on the warm-up suit stained with wine. He rifled through the purse for money. He took what he needed, then ripped open a chocolate bar and bit into it. He dumped it and the rest of the contents on the floor, hoping his wife would blame it on the cat. By the time his wife and son arose, he was long gone.

During his first class, the boys openly laughed at his newest disfigurement. They were impossible, wouldn't run through the easiest drills, until Tadeusz picked out a scapegoat and smacked him across the head. The news of his bad temper spread quickly to the rest of his classes, and the day became easier. Now that he was working half-time, he had two hours to relax before he met Mateusz, football in hand. After cake and tea at his mother's flat, Tadeusz took his son out to the football pitch. He set out orange cones he had borrowed from the school and tried to get his son to dribble around them. Mateusz refused. Tadeusz got so mad it took every ounce of willpower to keep from hitting his son, the way he had his student earlier in the day. He lit a cigarette and raised his collar to fight off the biting breeze. Mateusz kicked the ball into the first cone, knocking it over.

"Great!" Tadeusz said. "You want to kick, kick away." He threw the cones to the side and rolled the ball back to his son.

Mateusz took two steps back, pulled his lips taut, and laid into the ball. Tadeusz watched in amazement as it sailed well over the goal and crashed into the bushes behind.

"Jesus Christ," he mumbled.

"Jesus Christ!" he yelled, tossing away the cigarette. "Don't worry, I'll get it. I'll get it! Just stay there."

Running to the bushes, a good fifty meters away, was painful, what with the cold tearing into his lungs and his old knee injury. Gym teacher or no, Tadeusz was in bad shape to begin with. The run invigorated him, however. That's my son, he thought. And I'm his dad. How long had it been since he truly felt like a father? Maybe he hadn't felt this way since the little guy came into this world. Who would have thought, with his books and his piety, that he really is my son?

The ball lay deep in the bushes, whose branches whipped Tadeusz's face as he scrambled, first crouched over, then on his hands and knees, for his goal. He reemerged, ball in hand, only to find, once again, that his son had walked away.

...

"Son," Tadeusz said. "I'll do anything, just name it, anything, if you dribble that ball for me."

The next day, Tadeusz had again borrowed the cones and set them out on the pitch.

"You have a hell of a leg," he said. "No one could question that. But if you want to play, you have to learn how to move with the ball. That's the hardest thing to do."

Mateusz looked first at the ball, and then the line of cones.

"I'll do anything," Tadeusz repeated.

And this is how he found himself in the confessional booth, a place he hadn't visited in who knows how many years. Before he went in, he prayed to God that one of the younger priests of the parish had confession that day, but no, yet again, God let him down. The rector was humbling himself by hearing confession today.

Certainly the old bastard recognized Taduesz through the grate, if not by his voice. He came to the Styś household every year to calculate the tithe. Tadeusz was unlucky enough to always be around at that time. Last year, Tadeusz passed out during the customary dinner, at least that's what his wife said. But the rector never let on that he had a seriously fallen Catholic in his midst. He went through the preliminaries like he did with the old birds, Tadeusz supposed. Even though he had had the intention of serving up just a few harmless sins, Tadeusz found himself giving the priest the whole spectacle of his life: the adultery, the drinking, the swearing, even the anger he felt towards God about his father's death.

"To be honest, Father, I'm here for my son. I promised him that I would come here today."

The rector sighed, then said: "Sometimes children are God's greatest gift to the wayward, my son. They are innocent, pure, and they have not been out of God's midst for as long as we have. To come here for your child's sake is a good start."

"Thank you, Father."

He's not such a bastard after all, thought Tadeusz as he left the booth. He slid into a pew while Mateusz waited in back, with every intention of starting on his penance. However, he couldn't remember the prayers, not even a lousy "Hail Mary." He knelt anyways, pressed his hands together and went through the motions for a good fifteen minutes.

...

Tadeusz and Mateusz trained after school for the rest of the week. His son still wouldn't speak, but he didn't bolt every time Tadeusz turned his back, either. The kid was a bit clumsy around the cones. He might never be agile enough for a forward, like his old man, but with some weight on him, he'd make a great defender, and with his leg, Tadeusz envisioned deadly long passes downfield.

On Friday, the cold froze the sweat in their hair. They ended early, and as they walked quickly homeward, a city bus coughing black exhaust into their faces, Tadeusz placed his hand on his son's head and said:

"Maybe next time we could work on the chatter?"

To his delight, he felt his son's head slowly nod.

...

Instead of spending his night in a bar, Tadeusz stayed home that Friday night and watched television with his son. Someday soon, he promised, he'd have a satellite dish hooked up. If the boy were going to play for the Red Devils of Manchester, he'd have to learn English, wouldn't he?

In the morning, with All Saint's Day right around the corner, Taduesz wrapped up against the fierce cold and helped his mother clean his father's grave. After, he caught a bus to the Russian market and bought a warm-up suit for Mateusz with the money his mother had given him. He wanted his son to wear it today. Sure, it was cold, but his son would have to toughen up. Hell, they play football in Russia in the middle of winter. He rushed home, only to find that both his wife and son were gone. No note, not like in the old days. He knocked about the flat, nibbling on a heel of bread. The movies, he thought. Another bus ride back across town.

A whole pack of people were lined up in front of the theater. He checked the kiosk out front and saw that some American cartoon was playing. The door to the theater opened and the sheep began to pour in. He jostled through the crowd. Maybe he saw his wife up at the front. Surely Mateusz was with her. When he recognized his wife's boss he knew who was keeping him from his son this afternoon.

The bastard, he thought. Not only is he screwing my wife, he's taking away my kid, too. He sells fruit, for Christ's sake.

He took off his frazzled glove and pulled out the remainder of his money, pawing through the bills as if rubbing them would make their value increase. Sure, he thought, in the old days we didn't have these fancy American films, but at least a man could afford a ticket when he wanted one. When the last of the crowd had bought their tickets, Tadeusz put on his best smile and approached the box office. His battered face did not charm the old bird sipping her tea and munching on a sandwich. Before Tadeusz finished his plea, she pulled the curtain shut.

...

A widow who lived in a wooden house not far from Taduesz's block sold vodka out of her back door. Most of her customers arrived in the middle of the night, after the stores and bars closed, so she was surprised to see Tadeusz jump over her fence and did little to discourage her mongrel from snapping at his legs.

She was not the type of businesswoman to give out credit. She was lonely, however. Tadeusz secured a bottle after a couple drinks and a few laughs, plus a promise that he'd return someday soon, not only with the money he owed, but also with the intention of spreading some of his cheer into her bedroom. He grimaced as he left--the woman was in her fifties at least--and caught a bus to his favorite bar, which was housed in a sixteenth century cellar on the main square. It was a wine bar, but most of the men who drank there snuck in their own bottles and just bought chasers from the owner. Tadeusz broke out his bottle first, which ensured that he could stay hours on end, drinking at someone else's expense.

A Polish gentleman does not count his shots, nor look at his watch when he is in a bar, so Tadeusz had no idea of how much he had to drink, nor the hour, when Kasia's father strolled in. Tadeusz's first impulse was to duck into the toilet, or to leave the bar altogether, but both doors were between him and the man who had thrashed him, in public, in front of his son, just three weeks earlier. The man came right up to him. Tadeusz trembled. But instead of another blow, Kasia's father put his arm around him and poured out a drink.

"Ancient history," he said, before Tadeusz could say anything. "If Wałesa can befriend Kohl, I can befriend you!"

The vodka flowed. Sure, Tadeusz was chided a bit, both by his new benefactor and the other men that now surrounded him. But this was the way in the old days. A man insults another, a little blood is lost, but later, when both men realize there's no reason to go on like that, they share a bottle or two and put the past behind them. A little kidding is to be expected. Tadeusz was sure enough of his own manhood to contribute to the fun.

"You had me, that day, my friend," he said. "No doubt. But it was a fair and just fight. Let me tell you, though. My boy, who's going to be a star, by the way, didn't like to see his old man get the life knocked out of him."

This raised a new round of laughter, and another round of shots.

"He hasn't talked to me since!"

"And your wife?" someone asked.

"My wife?"

"She's getting a little life knocked out of her as well!"

"Power to her," Tadeusz shouted. "I can't even look at the hag any longer."

Laughter, shouting, drinking. The evening passed away. Tadeusz was driven to tears by these new, generous friends of his. At one point he slipped off his bar stool for a little breather, he was so overwhelmed. While he slumped on the sticky linoleum, all the voices around him gradually faded.

Something cold and wet revived him. He looked up to see snow cascading from the sky. It took him a moment to realize that he was now outside the bar. But why was he so cold? He had worn his down jacket. Not until he stood and leaned against the building did he realize that the only thing he had on was his underwear.

"Those guys," he murmured. "What jokers." He turned back to the bar but the door was locked and the lights were off. In fact, the whole square was dark. He wrapped his arms around his torso, only to discover that he couldn't bend his fingers. His toes were numb as well. He realized his predicament. The cold had sobered him a bit; his fear did the rest. He leaped through the park in the middle of the square. One taxi remained at the stand. Taduesz reached for the back doorknob, but it was locked. He pounded on the passenger window, his breath condensing instantly on the glass.

"Let me in!" he shouted.

The taxi driver reached across and cracked the window.

"Show me the fare," he said, crinkling the corners of his mouth.

"At home," Tadeusz said. "At home. Take me home."

"Buses start in an hour," the driver said. He started the taxi and sped off into the night.

Tadeusz looked one way, then another. Not a soul about. Every store, every house, dark. His whole body now numb. I'm going to die, he thought. His legs began to move. "I'm going to die," he said. As he ran through the streets, he repeated it, like a mantra: "I'm going to die. I'm going to die."

He turned left at an intersection, only to be met by a fresh gust of wind and snow.

"God help me, I'm going to die."

As his feet pounded the icy pavement, a thought came into his head that he could secure clothes from a Russian. Traders were about at all hours, dragging their bags of shit to cheap hotels or to the market. The train station stood at the end of the road he was now on, but no Russians were in sight. He quickened his pace. Some feeling returned to his limbs. Still, he kept up his mantra, even once he entered his block and huffed up the stairs. Only when he reached his floor did he fall silent and lean against the wall to catch his breath.

His son, his sweet son, wrapped in a blanket, sat on the floor in front of the door.

"What's this, little man?" Tadeusz asked. His lungs burned, he knew his lips were blue; the words barely made it out of his mouth.

Mateusz looked up. He didn't seem the least bit surprised by his father's sudden appearance, or his near nudity. He stood and opened the door of the flat. Tadeusz followed him in and immediately launched himself into bed, wrestling the covers around him, and pulling the pillow between his legs.

"I'll warm up some." Tadeusz croaked out. "Make tea or something."

His son threw another blanket over him and cranked up the space heater.

Mateusz always slept in the flat's one bedroom, with his mother. This night, he crawled in next to his father. Tadeusz didn't notice this, until the boy began to quietly sob. Tadeusz stirred, still suffocated with the cold the warmth of the bed just barely nudged aside. He opened his eyes and saw the tears stream down his son's plump cheeks. He heard a thump against a wall, then another. Thump followed thump, and soon Tadeusz recognized the sounds of his wife, the moans, the loud, quickening breath, of her making love. As the two in the adjoining room raced towards climax, little Mateusz hiccupped and gasped, and cried even harder.

On any other night, he would have had both the strength and the inclination to break down the door and beat both his wife and lover to death. Tonight he had neither. The sounds of his child and the sounds of his wife became entangled in his mind. He remembered his father's nocturnal desire to go "somewhere else," and as Tadeusz raised the pillow above his son's face, he realized that there was no better place to be.

BEER MONEY

In the early summer of 1990, just six months after the fall of the Berlin Wall, sixty American Peace Corps Volunteers arrived in Poland. Lech Walesa, the newly elected President, met with them in a ceremony marred by vague terrorist threats from a group of recently laid off policemen. Piotr watched the widely publicized event on television, gazed at the smiling, wide-eyed Americans in their bright clothes and friendly demeanors. Every day for weeks afterward, Piotr, instead of working on his dissertation, took the tram to the Peace Corps training site on the outskirts of Warsaw to watch the Americans on the other side of a high fence. They played volleyball, ate their suppers under the sun, smoked and talked loudly in their American English, a language Piotr had heard only on black market cassette tapes and the "Voice of America." Regardless of the weather, the Americans laughed and slapped each other's shoulders. They were always happy. Piotr had never seen such a large group of people exhibit such exuberance about living in Poland. He was in awe. He wanted to know their secret.

By the end of August, the group of Americans had dispersed across the country. Before they left, Piotr had plenty of chances to bump into one on the street and strike up a conversation, but the artificial nature of his intent tied up the English words in his throat. He hoped at least one would patronize his kiosk in the Palace of Culture market. Such an encounter demanded a verbal give and take. When no Americans came to the market, he decided to take his business to them; like many others seeking to take advantage of the "New Capitalism," he began selling beer on the trains waiting for clearance at the eastern station.

Instead of rushing through each train car and yelling "Piwa!" like so many of his counterparts, Piotr walked sideways down the aisle, very slowly, not only to accommodate his large size, but also to have the opportunity to smile broadly at prospective Americans. He never hurried, even though the trains remained at the station for only a limited time before moving on to Warsaw Central, or to Lublin or Terespol. His approach was hardly one to appeal to the heavy drinkers that populated the Polish trains day and night. But Piotr was not interested in having what he thought the dregs of Polish society as patrons. In fact, he rarely made it to the second class cars, opting instead to concentrate on first class, where most potential customers for beer did not sit. Americans always went first class.

The second weekend of September, Piotr was on the sparkling new Lublin-Gdansk Express, first class, car 10. As he was squeezing past the second compartment, an unshaven Pole with droopy eyelids tapped on the glass and pointed to the basket in Piotr's hand. Normally, Piotr would have ignored him, but inside the same compartment sat a woman whose eyes immediately locked onto his. She wore a yellow top that was nothing more than a tube-shaped, elastic-filled piece of cloth, a pair of baggy shorts that reached her knees, ankle socks with a small pink ball above the heel and a pair of white, pink-trimmed Nike sneakers.

American.

Across from her sat a man in his mid-twenties. His beard was untrimmed, his hair uncombed, and his black, poorly fitting clothes were probably purchased in one of the Russian markets that now dotted all the eastern Polish cities. Yet he wore a type of leather shoe unknown to Piotr and was reading a paperback of Joseph Conrad in the original English.

An American hoping to be mistaken as a Pole.

Piotr smiled. He thought of his brother-in-law who was at that moment in Belgium getting a small diamond fitted into one of his front teeth. Piotr had called him an idiot, but now he wondered about the advantage of having such an ornament. He slid open the door.

"Ile?" the droopy-eyed Pole said, touching Piotr's basket with a well-manicured hand. The upper half of his body slithered into the corner of the compartment, but his short legs were spread wide to utilize the space the other occupants were not using. His hair was unwashed, and he smelled a bit, yet he was wearing a Rolex and Italian shoes. He was probably drunk.

"Trzydziesci," Piotr replied, with undisguised disgust.

The Pole whistled through perfect teeth and held out a fifty thousand zloty note he had pulled out of a large wad that was bounded by at least one million zloty note.

"Dwa?" he asked without a hint of sheepishness.

Piotr heaved a big sigh before accepting the note for two bottles he had paid five thousand a piece for.

The Pole grabbed the bottles, pried the cap off one with his pinkie ring, and downed the whole half liter in one, slow draw.

The young woman shuddered and turned her eyes to the train platform outside her window. The man sitting across from her licked his lips then went back to his Conrad. The Pole dropped the empty bottle on the floor, closed his eyes and slid further into his seat.

"Good morning," Piotr said, in his best English. "Would the young lady and gentleman care for refreshment?"

"Oh!" the woman said. "You speak English?"

"Of course," Piotr said, bowing low to the woman. "May I?" he asked, gesturing toward the empty seat next to her.

"Oh, please do," the woman said.

Piotr had to step sideways through the door. He pushed away the outstretched legs of the Pole, who retreated into a fetal position.

"I'm Mary," the woman said, holding out her hand. "The grump sitting in the corner with his face in a book calls himself 'Rambo,' but don't believe that. I've been on the train for two hours and he's only said a few words to me. It's frustrating because I've hardly spoken English since I've been here and now I get on the train to find another American and he won't say a word to me. What's your name?"

"Piotr," he said, sitting down next to this charming woman. Ah, her smell! Whatever sweet scent she wore drifted in and out of his nostrils and sent shivers down his spine. Before she boarded the train she could have been rolling through wildflowers in the Tatra Mountains, for all Piotr knew. Her perfume was so unlike the vinegary swill his sister doused herself with every Sunday before Mass.

"Or Peter, in your fair language."

"Oh, I can hardly tell you're not a native speaker!" Mary said as she touched Peter's huge thigh with her impossibly small hand.

Rambo snorted.

"It's alive," Mary said. "If that uncouth sound you just made was directed toward me, Mister, you can save it for an Ugly American. I was expressing a professional opinion."

She turned back to Peter.

"I'm an English teacher," she said. "In Lublin." She handed him her teacher's identification booklet.

"Oh, but don't look at the picture!" she cried, snapping her hand around his. "Just that day my hair dryer blew out all the circuits in my block and I had to go to the photographer's in such a frazzle. Polish apartment blocks! I wish something could be done with the utilities. Telephone included. They keep telling me that I will soon be able to call America direct. I wish they would hurry. The gym teacher at my school, who, by the way, is a bit too wayward with his hands, if you know what I mean, said that just last year he had to call an operator in Koszalin, that's on the Baltic, isn't it, just to connect to his girlfriend who lived in the next block. Is that true, Peter?"

Peter leaned back, away from the barrage of dialogue. He was still dealing with this new word: "frazzled." If the woman would only let go of her i.d. he could look inside and see what it meant.

"That is, or was, the case, my dear lady," Peter said finally.

"What a crazy country!" Mary said, taking back her i.d. "Tell me, Peter. Were you ever in a gulag?"

The American man did not even try to hide his annoyance of his compatriot. He grumbled, shifted in his seat. He leafed through his *Under Western Eyes* so furiously that two pages tore loose and floated to the floor. Peter could only smile at the woman's incredible naiveté.

"No, my dear, the era of the gulag was before me," Peter explained. "But my grandfather...My poor grandfather! He spent three years at Siberia after the War. Up to this day five years ago, that is when he died, he slept with bread under his pillow, because he was afraid of not having food in the morning."

"Wait!" Mary said, shuffling through her backpack-sized purse. "I just love collecting such stories." She took a moment to scribble down a few sentences in a brand new, pocket-sized diary.

The young man slapped his book shut.

"I can definitely use a beer," he said.

Mary looked up.

"Don't worry, Princess. I'll speak in English so that you can follow along."

"Watch it, Mister," Mary said. "I get along okay considering I've only been here a short time."

"Yeah, whatever," the young man said. "The name's Ken. Nice to meet you, Peter. I believe you told the specimen in the corner that your beers go for thirty thousand?"

As he reached to give Peter the money, he winked at Mary.

"Duh, Mr. Einstein," Mary said. "Like numbers are so hard to remember."

Peter waved the money away.

"That is not necessary, my new friend," he said. "This money is nothing to me. If I may tarry here until the train reaches Centralna, to practice my English, this will pay for the refreshment."

That said, he wiped shiny a bottle with his pocket handkerchief and popped off the cap with his teeth.

"Oh!" Mary cried, throwing her open hands to her cheeks.

Peter flashed a big smile. Before handing over the bottle, he scrubbed the open end with the handkerchief.

"I thought they only did that in movies," Mary said, touching his leg once again. "Peter!"

"In Poland, my dear, anything is possible. It is very hot outside. Would you like one, on the house, you say?"

Mary had removed her hand from Peter's leg, but he could still feel her touch.

"Oh, I really shouldn't," Mary said. "It's only 2 o'clock. My friend is meeting me in the station and then we're going to the new grocery store near the Holiday Inn. I hear they have chocolate chips. Peter, have you ever had a real American, home-made chocolate chip cookie?"

"Jesus," Ken said. "Just accept the man's hospitality."

"Oh, gee," Mary said, tapping her small, finely painted lips with an equally small, finely painted fingernail.

"I guess just one wouldn't hurt," she said.

"Done!" Peter said. With great ceremony, he plucked a bottle from the basket and ran the handkerchief across the top, all the while he flexed the ample flesh around his right eye. With one hand he pulled back that flesh and held it against his skull, and with the other he lodged the bottle's top between eyeball and eye socket. When he felt the sharp tines of the bottle cap bite right behind bone, he flicked his wrist once, twice, and on the third try, through running tears and a black, blinding headache, the bottle cap gave and dropped into his lap.

"Oh my god oh my god OH MY GOD!" Mary had sprung from her seat, was spinning, twirling, pounding her bright white Nikes into the floor. "Peter!

"Where's my camera. I've got to find my camera." Next, she pulled her hard-shell Samsonite day bag from the shelf above the seats, began rifling through it, flinging a passport, deodorant, toothpaste, more balled socks and dainty underthings every which way.

Peter's eyes passed briefly over her underwear before resting on the passport.

"Do it again!" Mary yelled, spying Peter through her camera. "If I only had my video..."

"He's not a circus act," wide-eyed Ken said halfheartedly.

"A Pole never lets friends drink alone," Peter said. In his mind, he heaved a sigh, and even though the whole right side of his head ached, he took up another bottle.

Mary stood camera ready, Ken, mouth in an "O," rested his beer on his chin. Peter prepared bottle and eye socket in the same manner as before, but this cap wasn't as easy. While Mary "oohed" and "ahed" and clicked picture after picture, Peter flicked his wrist six, seven times, and when that didn't work he twisted the bottle deeper into his socket, all the time silently cursing his brother-in-law, "Diamond Tooth," for teaching him this ridiculous trick, cursing the machine which capped the bottle, cursing God for selecting him to be born in this country.

More tears, new headache on top of the old, but the cap finally gave. Instead of landing gracefully in Peter's lap, it flipped end over end across the compartment and bounced off the sleeping Pole's Rolex. Beer, shaken into foam, fountained out of the bottle and all over Peter's shirt and finely groomed hair.

"Peter!" Mary said.

"Jesus H. Christ," Ken said.

Always quick to regain composure, Peter wiped clean face and hair and raised the bottle to his companions.

"Na zdrowie!" he toasted, before downing what was left in the bottle.

"Na zdrowie," Ken and Mary repeated quietly, in unison, before taking small sips of their luke-warm beer.

All three were silent a moment. Peter thought he must look a mess. He became conscious of the sounds of other passengers entering the train, their over-sized bags sliding over compartment windows and catching on door handles. He should go and sell the rest of the beer, jump off the train maybe, before it pulled out of the station and headed for the center of Warsaw. He felt he had lost this audience. There were other Americans.

Mary, however, broke the silence, first by tapping a button on her camera, which began to rewind the film automatically with a faint whirr, then by asking a question which made Ken throw his hands up in the air:

"Peter, how did you get so big?"

Mid answer, the train finally began to move. At least twenty minutes late, Peter figured.

"My mother had difficulty finding food to keep me so fat, but she made sacrifices," he said. "She did not want to lose her son to the army. When I was at university there was no problem. Students are 'exempt,' you say? But while I waited for placement in English Philology department, for the Phd, there was a problem. So I ate..."

The train snaked toward the Vistula River. Peter paused to allow his companions to enjoy the view of Warsaw's Old Town, the way the birds circled the church spires and how the sun reflected off the Renaissance buildings in pastel flashes of pink, green and orange. He cautioned them not to open the window, however. It had been a dry summer in Poland; the river's wide banks were clearly visible. There was less water than usual to dilute the raw sewage pumped into the Vistula.

"Polish army does not want fat men, only thin boys," Peter continued. "We are a poor country. Our army does not have the money for the many foods I eat."

He laughed, a bit too loudly, he thought, but his two companions joined in.

"These chocolate cookies you talk about, Mary. I will eat them all up. I will eat all you bake with your pretty hands!"

They laughed and laughed until all three were wiping tears from their eyes.

"Shh," Peter whispered. "We will wake up the drunkard."

Mary covered her mouth, Ken hid behind an uplifted arm. The Pole had uncurled from his fetal position and was almost sitting up straight. Peter noticed that he slept with one eye only partly closed.

The train slowed as it began its descent into the tunnel which passed under the streets of Warsaw. The impending darkness cut short the muffled laughter of the Americans. Only Peter seemed to realize that the lights had not clicked on. Soon, the compartment was pitch black.

"It's so dark," Mary whispered.

"Ooh, I'm scared," Ken said in imitation of her high voice.

"Watch it, Mister..."

The absence of light seemed to awaken the drunken Pole. They heard a bag drop to the ground. Something was unzipped, something was rustled.

The train screeched to a sudden halt. Even though it had been moving slowly, Mary bounced into Peter's side.

She stayed against him and dug her sharp fingernails into his thigh.

"This happens often," he said, knowing full well that this was not the case.

A flash of light. The Pole was now standing in the still compartment and held a lit butane lighter in front of his face. Something was on his head Peter could barely make out. It looked like a gas mask, an old one, something straight out of a movie about the Uprising.

"My stop," the Pole said, in English, as he lit a cigarette. From his bag, he took what seemed to be an unusually long knife. The red glow from his cigarette's cherry danced along its edge.

"Now, money and passports," the man said, in a voice that sounded too friendly for a demand.

The dull emergency lights in the hallway flickered on. The thief indeed had a gas mask on his head. He held the knife casually while he smoked.

"Money and passports," he repeated in the same tone.

Screams and shouts began to permeate the rest of the car. Mary sat up straight, arms crossed. Her nostrils flared, her teeth were visible through parted lips, her stenciled eyebrows slashed downwards toward the bridge of her nose. Where Peter expected fear in her dark eyes he found coldness, anger. Opposite her, Ken was already folded into a ball, face hidden in his hands.

"Now see here, my friend..." Peter said, as he started to rise.

"Sit, fat man," the thief said, waving the knife near Peter's eyes. "Or I cut you like cookie."

Beyond the thief, a cloud of gas was fingering its way along the ceiling of the hallway. Tear gas, Peter thought. In Poland always tear gas.

"Money and passports."

Ken stopped cowering long enough to pull a neck pouch from under his shirt and toss it onto the thief's bag.

"Good American. Now, Playmate of the Month who talk and talk," the thief said, flashing his teeth at Mary.

"I don't think so," she said.

"No?" the thief said. "I have you, maybe?"

His knife never wavering from Peter's eyes, the thief reached for Mary. When she raised her arms to fend him off, he grabbed her tube top, right between her breasts, and twisted it in his hand. Fingers outstretched, she went for his eyes, but the thief simply twisted her top further, first pulling her to her feet, then sending her to one knee. Her right hand shot to her side and landed on Peter's thigh for support.

Do something, you stupid American, Peter willed of Ken. The thief was not that big. Between the two of them, they could easily strip him of knife and gas mask and toss him into the hall. Ken, however, was beyond help. He was visibly shaking. A circle of urine spread underneath him.

Peter could not combat the thief alone.

"Stay calm, Mary," Peter said. "I am giving this man your bag and your passport. These we can replace."

Mary didn't reply. She was rigid in the thief's hand and her eyes remained locked to his. Peter reached around her for her purse and passport, and dropped them into the thief's bag.

"Good," the thief said. "Smart Pole."

Peter took his day's profits from his shirt pocket. The outer bills were wet with beer.

"You keep Polish beer money, fat man," the thief said and chuckled. "I take your woman, no?"

The thief leaned into Mary, bringing his dry lips close to hers. She clenched her teeth against the impending kiss. But the thief just chuckled once again and threw her back into her seat. Her head hit the window with a thud.

"Next train ride, yes?" the thief said. He shoved his take into the bottom of the bag and zipped it closed, all the time keeping the knife on Peter, who still held the zlotys. The thief slid open the door. Gas trickled in. Whether it was out of habit, or courtesy to his victims, he closed the door behind him. In the hall, the gas swirling around him in yellow clouds, the thief bared his teeth once more before fitting the mask to his face and moving on to the next compartment.

Mary made a lunge for the door.

"Bastard!" she shouted. "You won't get away with this!"

Peter grabbed her around the waist.

"We must stay," he said. "The police..."

"Bastard!" Mary had her hands on the door handle.

"The gas," Peter said. "The gas!" With more force than he wanted to use, he yanked her fingers from the handle and flung her back into her seat.

"My purse," she said. "It's my purse." Her red eyes were beginning to tear from the gas.

"I will get it," Peter said. "You promise to stay."

"The bastard!"

Peter pinned her against the window and quickly tied his handkerchief around her nose and mouth.

"Keep shut your eyes," he instructed. "Keep shut your eyes."

Peter reached across and grabbed Ken's arm.

"You!" he said, pulling the still whimpering Ken on top of Mary. "Brave Rambo. You keep her. She stays here. You keep her!"

When Peter was satisfied that Mary could not squiggle free of Ken's grasp, he opened the door and jumped into the gas-filled hallway. Muffled pleas and stuttered coughing came from up and down the car. Peter bent low and held his arm to his mouth and nose. The gas tore at his eyes. As he shuffled slowly down the hall, he speculated that the thief was an out of work policeman, his skills as an investigator of political crimes no longer tolerated in the new Poland. Maybe he had gassed Peter and his classmates on the eve of Martial Law.

There were the Italian shoes, two doorways down. Peter took three steps, and then threw his entire body into a forward leap. The thief spun, knife raised. Peter tried to turn away from the blade, but it caught him in the biceps, plunging into muscle before stopping dead against bone.

Peter screamed, though at that moment he felt no pain. He was in mid-flight when the knife entered him, and this did not slow his momentum. He slammed the thief into the ground. Under Peter's crushing weight, there was a loud crack. Part of the thief's rib cage collapsed and Peter felt a sudden release of pressure in the thief's chest. The thief let out a loud expulsion of breath and dropped the knife into the open compartment he was about to rob.

Peter wrestled off the gas mask and fixed it to his own face. He rolled off the thief, who returned to the fetal position he had maintained earlier in his seat. Only after

Peter stood and scooped up Mary's purse and the thief's bag did the blinding pain from his wound hit him. He gasped, and then he squeezed the six-inch gash closed with one hand. With all his remaining power, he wound up and kicked the thief twice in the kidney.

At least one accomplice would be in the car, probably armed with something more deadly than a knife. Peter didn't want to chance that confrontation, but still, he crept down the hall to where the gas was thickest. Two more compartments down, and his foot nudged the canister sputtering tear gas. He pulled down the nearest window and heaved the canister across the opposing tracks.

Back in his compartment, Peter unbuckled the nylon handle from the thief's bag and used it to tie the door handle to the metal leg of the nearest seat. He pulled the door curtains closed, opened the outside window and began fanning out the gas that was trapped inside.

Mary and Ken were on the seat where Peter had left them. They held each other like school children. Apparently, the gas had choked off Mary's anger and subdued Ken's fear. Peter paused.

What astounding innocence, he thought. What glorious ignorance!

Blood pooling above the cuff in his left sleeve, he removed the gas mask and bent forward to gather their tear-stained faces to his breast.

THE WIDOWER

Jay woke with his heart racing and sweat trickling down his heaving, bare chest. The pillows, the sheet, the blankets. All were damp.

"You were dreaming," Urka said.

"No. I was barely asleep."

"You yelled in your sleep. You had a nightmare? Tell me. It was about her, yes?"

"Not really."

"I can stay longer. Will you?" She burrowed under the blanket and sheet and closed her eyes. When he didn't join her, she tugged his arm. "Tell me more about her."

Outside the bedroom door, Urka's nieces played. The youngest—Jay couldn't remember her name—pressed her open mouth against the frosted glass and belched. Both kids scrambled away, screeching.

"The kids want their room back," Jay said. He got out of bed and tugged on a sock. His big toe went through it. Urka laughed.

"I just bought these at the Russian market," he said.

"You are surprised they are no good?"

Jay didn't answer, just put on the rest of his wrinkled clothes and slid his feet into the slippers Urka's sister reserved for him.

"Marta invites you for dinner," Urka said.

"Another time. I have basketball, and I'm already gonna be late." He opened the door and peeked around the corner. The two girls sprang from the kitchen table and ran towards him.

"American!" they squealed in unison.

"That's me."

They laughed even harder and squeezed through the door, jumping into bed with Urka while she snapped on her bra.

"It's supposed to be even colder tomorrow," Jay said. "Can you give me a ride to school?"

"Of course," she said.

"I need some laundry done, too," he said. "If you don't mind."

"Yes, yes. I will even fix your sock."

He left Urka to her nieces. Her sister and brother-in-law sat at the kitchen table. When Jay walked into view Adam grinned and gave him a thumb's up.

"There is cutlet," Marta said. "You stay?"

"I'm sorry, but no," Jay said. "Next time. I promise." He placed the slippers in the basket next to the front door and pulled on his Timberlands. He had most certainly tracked in ice and snow, but Marta must have dried them off. Both Marta and Adam appeared to like him, and they didn't seem bothered by the fact that Urka and Jay used their daughters' bedroom for their trysts. Most likely Marta hoped Urka would leave her husband for Jay.

How long can I keep doing this, he asked himself.

...

A few months earlier, two weeks into the fall term, Jay lounged on the table at the front of the college's only classroom, which was smaller than his parents' kitchen back in Indianapolis. In order to get to the table he had to crawl over the students' desks. The college rented the room from a high school. It was in the wing for music and art classes. Out of tune pianos lined the hallway. Students pounded away at them all day, every day.

Even though there was a break between classes, all his students were back, some munching *paczki* or sweet rolls, what Poles referred to as "second breakfast." Just like hobbits, Jay thought. The students hoped he would teach them American slang during these breaks, and as the days shortened, and they grew less suspicious of his lackadaisical teaching style, they asked more and more questions about his life in Indiana. It was 1991, just two years after the fall of the Berlin Wall, before Americans swarmed into Poland, and other countries in Eastern Europe, looking for adventure and cheap beer. He was the first American most of them had met.

"Why are you here?" one of the Malgosias asked. Of the eleven female students, five were named "Malgosia."

"What do you mean?" Jay asked. "I'm in the Peace Corps. There are Peace Corps Volunteers all over the world. I just happened to come to Poland. I told you all this."

"Yes, but why? You don't like the army?"

"The army?"

"I saw in this movie *Animal House*. People in it say to join the Peace Corps and they don't go to the army."

"It's not that way anymore. There hasn't been a draft in a long time. I like your taste in movies, though."

"I don't understand. Why come to Poland? Why not stay in America where it is so nice?"

What else am I supposed to do with an MA from a second-rate university, Jay thought. This gave him two years to avoid the decision to go on for a Phd. Plus, there was the adventure and the cheap beer.

"It's hard to explain," he said.

"You should be married," another Malgosia said.

Pretty much every other female student nodded. The four males booed.

"I was married," Jay blurted out.

There were gasps all around.

"Is that why you are here, to avoid your wife?" Arek said. The other three men laughed.

The women shushed them.

"I *was* married. Not anymore."

"What is her name?" Malgosia II asked.

"Carrie," Jay said.

The students sounded the name out a couple times, like they did with any new vocabulary words he taught them.

"You are so young," the first Malgosia said. "25, yes? Why you leave this Carrie? She not cook for you? Maybe you should cook."

"I'm not divorced. I'm a widower."

Bozena, the quietest, yet strongest student in the group, loudly sucked in her breath. The rest of the students looked back at her. She said something quickly in Polish, and when they returned their gazes to the front of the room their faces were blank. A moment passed. Some of the students wrote in their notebooks while others moved their lips, mumbling repeatedly, Jay knew, "widower, widower, widower" until the word sank in.

"Maybe we should start our lesson," Jay said. The students didn't protest at all. That was new. Jay smiled. The students opened their grammar books and waited for his next words.

...

At lunch, in the cafeteria, not one of the high school teachers gave him the stink eye, as they had all term when he made it clear he'd rather eat with his students than with them at the designated teacher's table. One of the teachers, twice as old as Jay, at least, heavily made up and dressed entirely in purple, sauntered over, patted him on the shoulder and murmured something in Polish. He didn't understand it, but given the blushes among the Malgosias it was likely something lascivious. And before Jay left for the day, the director of the college pressed her sister's phone number into his hand.

"When you visit Warsaw, you stay with her," she said. "She loves Americans and her husband works in Libya. Call! A happy personal life means a happy professional life, yes?"

While he waited for the bus, Urka screeched to a stop in her Polski Fiat and offered him a ride home.

It took him a moment to place her. He had only met her once before, at an introductory meeting with the director at the beginning of the term. He had found her strikingly beautiful: bright green eyes, large and sparkling, small button nose, slightly pointed chin, all framed in a pixie cut. Like an elf, he thought. He remembered that the bottom button on her blouse at come undone. He found it endearing somehow, and for the months their affair lasted, he often noticed that she was always just a tiny bit disheveled. Sometimes her top didn't quite match her skirt, or one eye was more made up than the other, or there was a clear run in her panty hose.

He bent down and looked at her through the passenger side window. She's so out of my league, he thought. A ride's a ride, though. The bus back to his flat necessitated a change in the central square. Sometimes it took longer than a half hour.

"Yes or no," Urka said, pushing open the door. "The bus is behind me."

Jay shimmied into the porta-potty-sized Fiat. Once in he managed to sling his book bag into the backseat without hitting Urka's incredible face. Even though he wasn't tall, he had to bend his legs to get in the seat and still his knees barely cleared the cracked dashboard. As he reached for the seat belt, he twisted his neck to take in Urka. She smelled like what? Baby powder? Subtle and pleasant, not all like the noxious brew blanketing the woman who had patted his shoulder at lunch. All of Urka's buttons were in place, but right above her right knee a paper clip was snagged in her skirt. Before he could situate himself comfortably in the seat and latch the buckle, she slammed on the accelerator. Jay grabbed his knees.

"Holy shit!" he yelled.

"What?" Urka asked as she sped into the opposite lane to pass another Fiat, putting them in the direct path of an oncoming truck. With just a couple feet to spare, she swung back into the proper lane, narrowly missing a dog pissing in the gutter. Jay squeezed his knees into his stomach.

Urka sighed. "My husband and I are not happy. We do not sleep together any longer."

"Oh, God," Jay said, as they nearly sideswiped a taxi.

"Like so many Polish people, I was married too young..."

Through what appeared to Jay as one near death experience after another, Urka spilled out her guts in a calm, steady tone. Her husband managed the children's clothes store on the first floor of their house, but he often closed it for weeks at a time to "make business" in the Netherlands. When he was home he spent most of his day playing his guitar and singing songs. Unlike most Poles, he wasn't Catholic, but some kind of Born Again; Urka didn't go into details about it. At any one time, Urka tutored a dozen students privately. Many of the students at the college had been hers in the past. Now the college's school year had started, and she kept the private lessons, despite her responsibilities at not only the college but also at a secondary school across town. She also had her five-year-old to care for. Her husband couldn't be bothered with that, let alone cooking or cleaning. He had his songs to sing.

"My life is very full," she finished, "but I am very lonely."

They skidded to a stop in front of the rectory, a gargantuan, multi-winged structure with a red steepled roof and walls of red brick. The director of the college had told Jay that people in town called it "Malbork," after the Teutonic castle near Gdansk. Next to it stood the beginnings of the church, the walls just a few feet high. Nobody in the parish was pleased that the rectory was completed first. It benefited Jay just fine, however. The college rented a flat in the rectory for him that was far bigger than what most families in Poland had.

Jay swallowed stomach acid and grimaced. "Did I even tell you where I lived?"

"Everyone knows this."

"Oh, right."

Now that they were stopped, and his stomach was calm and he could look at Urka steadily again, he wondered how he should respond to her confessions, or if he should at all. When he first arrived in Poland in June, Urka's abrupt revelation about her love life would have shocked him, but not now. Right before the Peace Corps training ended, a Polish teacher drove Jay and two other volunteers to Warsaw to hear President Bush, who was speaking in the main square of Old Town. The teacher prattled on about how much she would miss teaching the classes. She hoped the Peace Corps would ask her back for the next group. She then looked at Michael, one of the other volunteers, in the rearview mirror.

"I don't want to miss you, Michael. I want you," she said, in a very serious tone.

"Excuse me?" Michael said.

"I want to have sexual relations with you."

"Well, gee, maybe we should talk about it another time."

"Why? You are leaving soon. Maybe the Peace Corps puts you far from me."

"Yeah, but this is awkward, with these other dudes here."

"Why? They are adults."

"Guys, can you help me out?"

Jay didn't know what to offer, and he didn't know how things turned out between the teacher and Michael. He was just glad when the interminable summer training ended. Besides the language lessons, the most interesting classes were with the cross-cultural trainer, a Phd student at Warsaw University. She had told them that, in her dormitory, "Everybody slept with everybody." Americans shouldn't be fooled by the "Church's propaganda." Most Poles had no problems with pre-marital sex, or extramarital affairs. Under Communism, sexuality was one of the few freedoms people had. The government couldn't control what they did with their bodies.

But she warned them, especially the men, not to take it for granted. She said that Polish women would show them a lot of attention. Many of them would just be looking for Green Cards. Polish women were still expected to marry, the younger the better. They will not just "give out free sex." Maybe to a Pole they would, like the women in her dorm, but not to an American. With us they will have high expectations. At one point during the summer, a Peace Corps nurse gave them an obligatory lesson about proper condom usage. "Virtually all the cases of AIDS in Poland have been attributed to dirty needles," she said, "but the other STDs? You name them, Poland's got them. We'll send you to the site with as many condoms as you can carry. Run out, and we'll mail to you as many as you want, no questions asked."

After, the cross-cultural trainer told volunteers that the Peace Corps was far more worried about unwanted pregnancies than diseases.

Jay's initial supply of condoms were packed away, untouched, with Band-aids and Pepto and whatnot in the large blue plastic box given to each volunteer.

Urka looked at him patiently.

"You drive like a bat of out hell," Jay said.

"I have heard this expression 'bat out of hell.' It means 'really fast,' yes. I don't understand. Why are bats in a hurry to leave hell? Don't bats like hell?"

"I see your point."

Jay reached back for his book bag, lightly brushing Urka's cheek with the back of his hand. It made him shiver.

"Well, thanks for the lift," he said.

"The what? 'Lift?' Like an elevator?"

"No." Jay laughed. "It just means a 'ride.'"

"Oh, I see, *Pan* Professor. 'Gotcha,' yes?"

"Exactly, *Pani* Professor."

"I will learn a lot from you," Urka said. "I live over there. I can almost see my home from here. You need anything, you come to me, yes?"

She smiled and leaned towards him. He thought she might have expected a kiss. He might have done it but for the nasty acidy taste in his mouth.

After she sped away, he walked slowly up to the front door of the rectory. Why now, he thought? When we first met she had paid little attention to me. What was all this about?

And then he remembered. What he had said to the class. That he was a widower. For some reason that had spurned her on, and likely his director and the teacher in the cafeteria.

Well, that's crazy, he thought. Why would that attract her? Maybe she wasn't coming on to him. Maybe she was just being nice and friendly.

Tomorrow he should probably tell everyone that he wasn't serious, that he had never been married.

He just made it up.

...

The next morning, as the bus meandered its way towards school, he thought of a lesson. The students could interview each other and then after, write up imaginary obituaries. The whole widower thing was just preparation, he'll tell them.

Wasn't perfect, but it was all he could come up with.

When he got off the bus, Arek was waiting for him.

"Pan Professor," he said, "you like basketball?"

"It is a religion where I come from," Jay said.

Arek just looked at him and scratched an ear. "You like it then?"

"Very much."

Arek smiled and looked relieved. He told Jay his uncle was a custodian at his old high school—the same one Urka taught in, Jay would realize later—and it was possible for them to play in the gym evenings and weekends. They could even use the showers afterwards. Jay was thrilled. Arek promised enough players for a good game.

Outside the classroom stood one of the Kasias. She looked nervous, swaying some and biting on her thumb. Arek smiled at her and nodded, which seemed to put her at ease.

"Pan Professor..." she started.

She and two other students were from Warsaw and lived in a dorm. Every Wednesday evening they went to the one decent restaurant in town. Wouldn't he join them? They could practice their English, or he could practice his Polish. Whatever he wanted.

Jay had spent many an evening bored. He had a television in his flat, but no cable; there were only two channels. Most of the Polish shows were either talk shows, or tapes of Polish children lip-synching to popular American music. Occasionally an American sitcom would air, or maybe even a movie, but they were dubbed over, not with actors, just one guy repeating the dialogue in Polish. You could still hear the original English underneath. Since Jay's grasp of Polish remained meager, he pressed his ear to the television's speaker, anything to hear the scraps of English beneath the monotone Polish. When nothing American was on, he mindlessly pressed the button that changed the station, back and forth, back and forth, sometimes twenty times in a row. Occasionally good movies showed at the town's theater, a repurposed Jewish synagogue. It was a bit of a crapshoot. To prolong the life of the projector's bulb they'd only show the film if at least eight people bought a ticket. A couple of times Jay waited fruitlessly next to the box office window, mentally willing pedestrians passing by to come inside.

"That sounds wonderful," Jay said. "Thank you so much."

Kasia reddened and skipped into class.

Perhaps they think I'm sad, Jay thought, and they just want to keep me here. No one really seemed to understand why an American would give up two years of his life to live in Poland. At least five other volunteers from his training group apparently couldn't figure it out either; they'd already ETd, or "Early Terminated."

He decided to scrap the whole obituary thing. So they thought he had a dead wife. Is that such a bad thing?

...

A couple weeks later, the night before Halloween, the students arranged a costume party at a just opened café. "We love American holidays," one of the Malgosias said. "Polish holidays are so boring. Boring old men reading boring speeches. It is so boring!"

Jay pulled the sheet off his bed and wrapped it into a makeshift toga. When he first moved in the rectory's housekeeper gave him a houseplant. He sawed off some of the leaves and fashioned them into a laurel. At the party he survived his first real Polish drunk, matching Arek shot for shot. After five, Arek slapped him on the back and said he was becoming a real Pole. Jay vaguely remembered lecturing on the genius of Larry Bird and dancing to Polish techno, and kissing a bunch of women there, students and otherwise. And Urka. But not much more than that. He couldn't even remember how he got home.

The next evening he was trying his best to appreciate a cassette his baby brother had sent. Nirvana, it was, a new band some people were crazy about. Someone knocked on the door, which gave him an excuse to turn off the tape.

It was Urka.

"Is it a bad time?" she asked.

"Not at all. Would you like to come in?"

"Of course," she said.

He told her he was expecting a telegram from a Peace Corps buddy. They were hoping to meet with some others for Thanksgiving. Since volunteers had no phones, telegrams were the only way to remain in contact. They were delivered at all times of day by strange men in street clothes.

"We cheat a bit, I'm sorry to say," Jay said. "They charge by the word, so we combine them since the people at the post office can't read English."

"No one will come tonight. Tomorrow is All Saint's Day," Urka said.

"Oh, right."

She wandered around his flat and read the post it notes he had plastered all over the place. On each was written the Polish word for the object.

"Does it help?" she asked.

"I don't know," he said. "Polish is like Martian."

"Our President Walesa might agree. His Polish is terrible."

"I've heard that," Jay said, "*Herbata?*"

"*Prosze.*"

Jay's kitchen was equipped like a dorm room: a compact refrigerator as loud as a freight train, a two-burner hot plate and an electric kettle. As the water boiled, he sliced a lemon. He had bought a tea set at a small department store in the center of town. The teacups were small drinking glasses you inserted into decorative metal holders. The set came with a tray, a sugar bowl and small matching plates. When he placed the tray on the table, complete with packaged cookies, Urka said,

"You drink vodka like a Pole. Now tea."

"I just have to start smoking and my conversion will be complete."

"Please don't," Urka said. She unpacked the plastic bag she had brought: carrots, mushrooms and a half dozen eggs still spattered with bits of feathers and goo.

"From my mother," she said.

"Umm. Thanks?"

Urka laughed, revealing a smudge of lipstick on a front tooth.

"She is a doctor," she said. "In Poland medical care is free, but my mother has so many patients. If they want good treatment, they give her things. Too much for her, too much for me, so now for you."

"Thank you. And thank your mother. If I ever get sick I'll bring her some M&Ms."

Urka sipped her tea. "Too hot."

She wandered over to the easy chairs in front of the television. Like his bed, they flipped open on hinges to reveal storages spaces. They weren't very comfortable. Jay had stacked a bunch of paperbacks on one.

"You must like Charles Dickens," Urka said.

"I guess. There's not much choice of novels in English here and they're kinda expensive. His books are long. More pages per zloty."

She nodded and turned back to the books.

"You kissed me at the party last night," she said.

"I think I kissed everyone at the party. Even Arek. I was drunk."

"Can I take this one?"

She held up a copy of Amy Tan's *The Joy Luck Club*. Jay's mother had sent it to him; he hadn't gotten to it yet.

"If you want."

"You also said my *dupa* was the reason why Michelangelo became a sculptor," she said.

Jay's mouth went dry. "Did I?"

Her back to him still, Urka reached down and oh so slowly lifted her skirt. When the edge of the wool reached the bottom of her cheeks she paused for a moment, before sliding it up to her waist. She wore nothing underneath.

She looked back over her shoulder, revealing just the profile of her face.

"Still think so?" she asked.

...

Over the next month Urka visited once or twice a week, usually without warning. She wouldn't stay long, typically darting off soon after they had sex, often leaving behind his freshly laundered clothes or supplies from her mother's larder. Once she showed up with pictures of an apartment in a typical Stalinist building, the walls bare cinderblock.

"You can live there cheap," she said.

"Why in the world would I do that? I live here for free."

"Maybe the school will pay..."

"This place is great, Urka. Look at the size of it. It's quiet, it's safe, and the priests don't bother me at all."

"They bother me," she said. "They look at me like I'm *kurwa*."

"Fuck'em."

A week passed and she didn't show up at all. The next day in school she told him the Probost, the head priest, wouldn't let her into the rectory. If she came again, he said, he would pay a visit to her husband.

...

How long can I keep doing this?

As soon as Jay opened the front door of the apartment building a gust of wind blasted him, stinging his eyes. He instantly regretted not staying for dinner. Marta always laid out a nice spread. Not too far away, though, a taxi idled at the stand, so he wrapped himself up and sprinted over. He never had to give the address to the taxi driver; he'd just say "Malbork" and the guy would chuckle and drive off to the rectory.

Despite the weather, all six of them showed up for basketball. Filip sported a new pair of sneakers, some kind of knock-off brand he probably bought at the Russian market. The other guys oohed and ahhed. The sneakers were shiny white, and at least looked expensive, but as soon as he ran out onto the court, the sole of one of them detached itself completely. He shuffled back to it with only an upper and black sock on one foot. Jay and the rest burst out laughing.

Filip wasn't so amused. His reddened face strained. It looked as if was going to cry. He tore off the other shoe and threw both it and the remains of its match to the other side of the gym. He announced he was going home. Arek offered to buy him a beer after the game. He huffed and puffed, but still slid on his street loafers and joined them on the court.

At one point, late in the session, Jay drove towards the basket but was immediately met with a double team. Caught on his pivot foot, and no passing lane open, he flung the ball over his head. It inexplicably went in.

"Nothing but net," Arek said.

There was clapping too, and a little yelp. All of the players turned and looked at Urka, who was standing in the doorway.

"Ah, your girlfriend, yes?" Filip laughed and elbowed him in the chest. "Little pussy," he said. "Little pussy."

The others snickered.

They finished the game. Urka stayed through the shower.

"You shouldn't be here," Jay told her in the hallway.

"I wanted to see you."

"We just saw each other."

"So?"

"All these guys know now. Eventually your husband is going to find out about us."

Urka shrugged.

Just end it, Jay thought. Do it now.

"That's your business," he said, turning away. "I'm going home."

She put her fingers on his arm. "No, you are not."

He turned back to her.

Not too far away, on the other side of an open door, Arek and Filip were on their knees, wiping away the black marks left from Filip's shoes with wet paper towels. Meanwhile, Jay dropped to his and buried his head in Urka's crotch.

...

By and large, Jay's students respected his "grief." They rarely asked about Carrie. Urka rarely did, either.

For Jay, though, the false memory grew in his mind. The more he thought about it, the more detailed and complete it became. He actually did know a Carrie, at least for a little while. They were in the same British Lit survey one summer. She wore the skimpiest little sun dresses. Drove him nuts. He was never brave enough to talk to her. That didn't stop his imagination. Sometimes he even dreamt about her and it woke him up. Her imaginary death often appeared to him, in various versions of this:

They meet in their first year at Indiana University in Bloomington and marry the week after graduation. Carrie's parents bankroll their honeymoon: two weeks in New England and Nova Scotia. On Cape Breton, after a few days of eating lobsters and cod sandwiches, of hiking every marked trail they come across, of fighting wind and rain, they find themselves on a narrow road at the very northern tip of the island, where they hope to stay at a small inn they read about in their *Frommer's*.

The accident happens when they are still miles away.

Jay wants a Coke from the cooler in the back seat of the rental car. Carrie turns to reach for it, but she can't get to it without first undoing the belt. So there she is, between the two seats as she fumbles for a can amongst the melted ice and cups of yogurt. Meanwhile, Jay steers with one hand and fondles her ass with the other.

"Keep it up, Mister," she says, "and that's all the play…"

These are the last words she ever speaks, for then there is an oncoming pickup truck, a squeal of tires, a slamming of brakes, and finally a shower of glass. When the car comes to a stop in the ditch on the side of the road, Jay's long, whitened fingers have gripped the wheel so tightly his nails punctured the skin right above the wrists.

He looks over to the passenger side.

"Are you okay?"

He sees her. He knows she is there.

Carrie tilts her head and smiles slightly. It is a smile not of amusement, but of resignation. She doesn't answer his question. They sit and look at each other. Waiting. He doesn't know for how long. He doesn't tear his gaze away until the truck driver raps his knuckles on the window.

"Are you okay? You need to come out of there, sir."

Jay blinks. He nods and acknowledges the other driver. Only then does he feel the ocean breeze blowing on his face. Then he sees the blood, and the bits of hair and cloth caught on the broken teeth of what remains of the windshield. He looks back to the passenger seat, to see again that resigned smile. It's empty but for bits of broken glass.

…

Jay picked the raisins off his sweet bun and popped them into his mouth. He poked between the folds of the bun in case he'd missed one.

"I don't understand," Malgosia said. "Why eat this way? There are buns with no raisins."

"I like buns and I like raisins," Jay said. "Just not together." He quickly scarfed the bun before shoving his hands back into his pockets. Like his students he still wore his winter coat. Apparently the high school had rented the college the coldest room in the building.

"What did this Carrie look like?" Malgosia asked, wiping crumbs from her chin.

"I'd rather talk about second breakfast options."

"Was she good looking? Show us a picture."

"I don't have one with me."

"What hair color?"

Jay thought back to British Lit. He typically sat in the row behind her, on the right side.

"Brown," he said. "Very curly."

"Was she pretty like Professor Kowalska?"

Jay paused. Half the students looked at him expectantly, the others down at their desks, as if embarrassed.

Did they know about Urka? Had Arek told all of them? Or someone else he played basketball with? Does her husband now know?

"There are many beautiful women in Poland," he said.

"You should marry Professor Kowalska," Malgosia said.

"I don't think her husband would go along with that."

"No problem."

All the students were whispering now. Except Bozena. She quickly made the sign of the cross and buttoned up the top of her coat.

"Perhaps we can get started again," Jay said.

"She is older. That is okay," Malgosia said. "Men die sooner than women, yes? This way you die together. It is very romantic."

Bozena hissed something at her in Polish. Malgosia frowned and threw up her arms.

"Don't listen to her," she said. "We want you happy. That is all."

"Why thank you. I want you to be happy, too," Jay said. "Now where were we…"

"You marry Professor Kowalska and we be happy. You stay all two years and more. We graduate with you. You happy. She happy. Everyone happy!"

Maybe just the class knows, Jay hoped.

Before lunch, one of the high school teachers, a man Jay had never spoken to, wrapped his meaty arm around his shoulders and shouted, "You are full man!"

So not just the class.

It was bound to get out. Biala Podlaska wasn't a big town, and Jay, as the only American, was news. Earlier in the school year he was even interviewed on local television. How long before Urka's husband came pounding on his door? Would the priests turn him out?

At basketball, he was morose and quiet. He couldn't buy a basket and he didn't joke with the guys in the locker room.

Perhaps to appease him, Arek arranged a day out in the woods for the following Sunday. Fresh snow had fallen, and a family friend owned some horses and a sleigh. He and his parents picked Jay up in the morning. Urka was in the back seat waiting for him.

I guess they don't care either, Jay thought. What a strange country this is.

They drove out to a nature preserve on the River Bug, the border between Poland and Belarus. Mikhail, the caretaker of the preserve, a giant of a man with long hair and thick black beard, immediately pulled Jay into an embrace.

"My new American friend!" he shouted.

Before the sleigh ride they fortified themselves with brown bread, homemade pickles, and kielbasa roasted on sticks over a bon fire, washing it down with a breakfast vodka, according to Arek's mother, one mixed with egg yolks and cream. For once the sky shimmered a clear blue and the sun shone brightly just above the bare trees. Long-legged dogs, coats as black as their master's beard, frolicked in the snow, occasionally bounding, tongues wagging, toward the fire to pounce on fallen kielbasa. Beyond the low, wooden house with gabled roof and stone chimney, the horses neighed and snorted, setting off the cows and pigs, even the chickens.

Stomachs warm with food and vodka, the old folks, with Jay and Urka as honorary members, slid under thick, woolen blankets, while Arek and some of the other students (a Malgosia, a Kasia, Artur and Magda) tied toboggans onto the back of the sleigh, and off through the woods they slid and sliced, bells jingling, bare trees creaking. More drink, always more drink, something hot this time from a dented thermos. Occasionally Mikhail reached for a branch and snapped it back, showering his cackling passengers with powdery snow. When the light began to fail single stars twinkled awake between the branches of the trees. The sleigh made its way along the riverbank and under the shadow of rickety guard towers left over from the war, then back through the trees and onto the house. They stomped in, shaking away snow and ice, laying saturated gloves and hats in front of the fire crackling and spitting in the stone hearth.

Mikhail's wife waited with a cauldron of tripe soup, platters of roast veal, sided with mountains of boiled potatoes covered in butter and parsley, more pickles, more bread and more drink, always more drink. Over the steaming plates, Mikhail regaled them with tales filled with heroic but full-hardy patriots, and the awful fire fights between Russians and Germans while starving Poles huddled in bombed out houses, and earlier, the crazy Polish king who took target practice on the bison he ordered launched from catapults.

"Raining bison! Can you imagine the idiocy? Is it any wonder why Poland was cut into three pieces?" Mikhail said. Then the top half of the kitchen door creaked open, and there were two horses, bobbing and neighing. Mikhail jumped up, cursing.

"To hell with you," he shouted, jumping from his chair. "Shoo! This is no place for you, beasts of burden. Out!" When he reached them he slipped apples into their mouths, cooing and brushing their snouts.

He came back to the table with new bottles of Zubrowka, the vodka infused with bison grass, plucked, he said, from fields just a few kilometers away.

All the guests squeezed together around a rustic table made of thick-cut planks. Jay held Urka's hand underneath, as he had for most of the day. Others began telling stories. Artur's grandfather had been sent to Siberia. After he returned to Poland, every night he put a piece of bread under his pillow just to make sure he had something to eat in the morning. Kasia's great grandfather, a colonel in the Polish army, was executed at Katyn in 1940. Magda's great aunt contracted syphilis when gang raped by Russian soldiers after the war. Before committing suicide she had unprotected sex with every Russian and Polish Communist she could find. There were stories of priests tortured by the Nazis, of unborn children cut from the bellies of mothers, of whole extended families locked into barns and burned alive.

When things got too dark, the stories switched to more recent history, to everlasting lines for anything that might be for sale in the shops, of too many residents in too small flats, of exchanging mimeographed copies of banned books, of romantic trysts in the Museum of Communism because it was one of the few places you wouldn't be disturbed.

The stories were related for Jay's benefit, he knew. In a lull he thought he should contribute, but what did he have besides an imaginary dead wife? So he told the group about hearing George Bush in Warsaw.

"I had to come to Poland to see an American president," he said. "He was the first American president to ever come here, yes?"

"It was very special to many people," Mikhail said.

"So many people were crying," Jay said. "Especially the babcias. For Bush? Cracks me up."

"There was hope he change the visa requirements for Polish people," Arek said.

"Bah!" Mikhail stood and poured more shots of Zubrowka. "Too many people want to leave Poland. The smart people leave, and the neo-Nazis stay. Do you know, my good friend Jay, about Kosciuszko and Pulaski? They fight in your revolution, eh?"

Jay nodded.

"Pulaski die there, yes? Such idiocy! And still Polish people want to go to America. You get Kosciuszko and Pulaski. You give us Madonna and McDonalds. Ha!"

"And Jay," Urka said. "They give us Jay. For two years."

"My good American friend. How do I forget!" Mikhail reached across the table, grabbed Jay's head and gave him a big sloppy kiss, right on the lips.

"To Jay," Mikhail said, raising a shot glass. "*Na zdrowie!*"

And so while the horses chuffed in the kitchen, they drank, and ate, and laughed even more. On the way home, before he fell asleep against Urka in the back seat, Jay thought about the question Malgosia had asked him one day in class: "Why are you here?"

For days like this.

...

The next Sunday Adam's father was celebrating his Name Day, so the whole family went off to Lublin, leaving Urka and Jay the run of their flat. They were lounging on the couch, naked under itchy, woolen blankets. The remains of the meal Urka had cooked—stuffed cabbage, boiled potatoes, leek salad--were scattered on the coffee table.

"Marek is with his father?" Jay asked.

Urka shook her head. "My parents."

"Of course."

"My husband was a good man, when he was young," Urka said.

"That's why you married him, I suppose."

"Yes."

They were once political activists. They met in high school, during the darkest days of martial law. After school, into the 1980's, she had been briefly imprisoned, her husband three times. The third time he languished for five months, even though no formal charges had been filed against him. They were married by then, and Urka was pregnant with Marek.

"There was a man," Urka said, "a Communist official. He was old and fat and sat behind this big desk. Some friends tell me this old fat man had power. I should petition him. So I went to this office. I wore a tight shirt so he can see my pregnancy. I begged and cried. He said nothing, this man. I thought I failed. But then he stands up and comes to me. Still he says nothing. He stands right in front of me and pulls down his trousers and waits for me. Silent. Doesn't ask. Just waits."

"Holy shit," Jay said.

"My husband is out of jail the next week. But he is different. He is not the same man I fell in love with. Now Marek is everything."

It's time, Jay thought. Just tell her. He lied. He'd never been married. But he didn't. He sat in silence. The sound of cars out on the street seemed very loud, as did the ticking of the clock on the wall above the television. Instead of confessing and begging Urka for pardon, he silently allowed the story he had woven to expand:

After his Peace Corps stint, he visits Carrie's gravesite on the anniversary of her death. Her parents and Ann, a younger sister, are there. He waits at a distance. He hasn't even talked to them since the funeral. The three stand there quietly. Suddenly, Jay's one time mother-in-law lets go of her surviving daughter's hand and lunges for the gravestone. She hugs it, sobbing loudly. Carrie's father does nothing to stop it, but even from this distance, Jay can see the man waver. He then simply collapses, like he's been shot. He too begins to sob, lying there on his side. Perhaps to stifle the cries, he buries his face in the freshly mown grass of his daughter's grave.

Ann still stands. For no apparent reason—Jay is deathly quiet—she looks in his direction. He quickly ducks behind a tree, breathing heavily. While he allows his breathing to slow, he stares down at the cheap bouquet of flowers he bought at the supermarket on his way to the cemetery.

Urka had picked up the television remote.

"Sometimes I don't think I ever really loved her," Jay said. "Carrie, my wife."

Urka raised an eyebrow.

"But you still marry her?"

"I was young. You were young when you got married, too."

Urka nodded and looked at Jay.

When he said no more she clicked on the television. The Olympics were on. Dorothy Hamill and some guy Jay didn't recognize talked into microphones, but whatever they were saying was dubbed over in Polish. Certainly it was about women's figure skating. Jay had read in his *Newsweek* that either Tonya Harding or Kristi Yamaguchi would win the gold. As soon as Jay remembered this, they showed highlights from Yamaguchi's routine.

"This woman won the gold medal," Urka said.

"That's good," Jay said.

"Why?"

"I don't know. She's nice. I like her."

"But she is not an American," Urka said.

"What are you talking about? Of course she's American. She's as American as me."

"But look at her. She's not like you. She's a China girl."

"What the hell are you talking about?"

"What?"

"You know nothing about my country."

"I was joking," Urka said. "What do you Americans say? 'Lighten up?'"

"Besides, Kristi Yamaguchi is of Japanese descent."

"Yes, sir." She took a magazine and started leafing through it, humming a tune that sounded familiar to him but couldn't quite place.

"Excuse me," he said. "I have to use the bathroom."

Naked, he padded across the cold floor. In the bathroom he waited for a few minutes before flushing the toilet he didn't use. He scrubbed the smells of dinner from his hands and the dried semen from his dick. He splashed his face with water and studied himself in the mirror. He looked the same as he always did: receding hairline, beady little eyes and an infected blemish on his neck that just wouldn't go away.

He left the bathroom and went into the nieces' bedroom. The sheets and pillows were strewn all about, and clothes were twisted in them. Jay found his underwear and a sock. He put them on but had no luck finding the other sock. He sat on the edge of the bed. Urka was still humming that tune, louder than the television.

While she was in prison, he thought, I was in my parents' basement, pulling bongs and listening to Genesis on the headphones. When she was bribing some Commie bastard with a blow job, I was feeling up a girlfriend or jacking off to a *Penthouse*.

How can I ever compete against that?

He couldn't. Maybe it didn't matter. His life had flowered open. He had his Wednesdays at the restaurant, and basketball games, and all the time he met interesting new people like Mikhail. Poland was a wondrous place. He could extend his two years' Peace Corps service to three, to be with his students when they graduated.

Urka continued to hum. Urka, sweet little Urka, his elven princess. He loved her. He knew. Just then he knew. He didn't care about her husband, or her son, or whether or not she was looking for a Green Card. Even his deception. All could be overcome. He had so many years ahead of him. With her.

He peeled off his underwear and his one sock and went back to the living room. He finally recognized the tune and sang along: "Oh Oh Oh Ohhh Oh, Little China Girl…"

"You like that song, too?" Urka asked.

"It's good, but no 'Warszawa,' mind you."

"Ah, Bowie's Berlin period. Not so easy to hum. He did a lot of drugs then."

"You are a very interesting woman, Urka."

She smiled and lifted up the sheet. He crawled back in next to her. The Olympic coverage had shifted to skiing.

"There's skiing in Zakopane?" Jay asked.

"Of course."

"We should go there. We can stop in Cracow. Maybe make a week of it. You can bring along Marek. I'll have to get to know him eventually…"

"Jay."

"But I guess it'll be too late for skiing once classes are out. But hiking, right? We can rent a cabin in the…

"Jay," Urka said, a little louder this time. She had taken his hand and was patting it. The sheet had fallen away from her shoulder, revealing her right breast.

"You must understand," she said. "This is it. This is all we get. Please tell me you understand."

AMBER

In 1974, Poland was rich beyond our dreams. Shops stocked plenty of meat, and bananas could be had every other week or so, not just at Christmas. My father surprised me one day with a real leather football, and much to his astonishment, he was given the opportunity to buy a Polish Fiat two years before his due. Gone, we thought, were the hours of waiting in line, hoping to be one of the lucky few to buy a plastic wastepaper basket, a dishtowel, a can of peaches, or whatever else was available that day. Even though so much could be bought--and buy we did--my parents, courtesy of their newly enhanced salaries, saved enough money for a summer long holiday, the first and last of my life. Less than a week after the school term ended, we packed the finely waxed Fiat and headed west, to the Mazurian Lake district, where we rented a cabin in a four-family compound.

Taking advantage of my father's good humor, I had insisted that he invite two of his colleagues, since their children, Alexander and Pawel, were my closest friends. The fourth cabin housed a mother and daughter, ethnic Lithuanians from the wild lands near Suwałki. The funny way they pronounced Polish, stretching back their lips and elongating the syllables to near breaking point, mesmerized my friends and me when we thought the only other language in the world besides our own was Russian.

My friends and I instantly latched on to Edita, the daughter, who was one year older. Day after glorious day we trailed behind her limber body, our eyes wide for her round hips and budding breasts. I wonder now if there could have been a sexual pull initially; my friends and I were at least a year away from the embarrassment of male puberty in school classrooms, how we would wear our omni prescient erections in our loose trousers the way a cabinet maker carries a hammer in his apron, yet we followed nevertheless, unconsciously loping after her around the lakes of Mazuria like puppies first learning to walk.

Each morning Edita stormed into our cabins while our parents slept snug against the cool early air. When she said, "let's go," we went, leaving behind the promise of hot tea with honey, blood red tomato slices dotted with minced onion, and fresh farmer's cheese atop bread still warm from the bakery on the lake's shore. Our minds remained bleary for the first few moments only. Soon enough we saw this world of water and birch trees through the eyes of Edita. She could name the different flocks of birds that pecked at the insects in the high grasses, and knew where to find the patches of sweet raspberries and wild strawberries our summer neighbors had missed on their gathering excursions. My father, with all his East German fishing rods and lures, more often than not returned empty-handed at the end of the day. Edita fashioned a rod from green wood she slashed from a pine tree and a three-meter length of twine. She baited the hook with dried curd and dropped it nonchalantly into dark, hidden pools where no boats could anchor.

"There's no fish there," I told her, the first time. She raised an eyebrow and grinned. Five minutes later, a three-kilo perch broke the surface, its throes of imminent defeat splashing the rolled-up cuffs of our trousers with water.

Before Edita muscled the fish out of the pool, she let her pole dip to the surface so that the perch swam hard for the channel to the lake. There, she said, it would lose its remaining strength fighting the currents surging in from the larger body of water.

"Go get some wood," she directed Aleksander and Pawel.

As she slapped dead a mosquito on her sun-burned neck, she bashed in the head of the now landed, still flopping perch with a large, flat stone.

"Not there!" she called to the wood gatherers, even though she couldn't see where they were. "Go to the fallen tree we passed this morning."

"But there is plenty of wood closer than that," I said.

"It's too wet," she said, without impatience. "The thicker the trees the more protection there is from the rain."

She placed the tip of her bone-handled knife into the sperm hole and sliced the fish up to its jaw. She tore out the guts with her bare hand and tossed them into the bushes we had just stripped of raspberries. I followed her down a path to a cleared area on the lake's edge, which gave us a view of our cabins across the shimmering waters.

"Rip out the grass," Edita told me. "Make a circle of bare dirt about a meter in diameter."

She left me to my task to gather pine needles. She returned with Aleksander and Pawel in tow, wood of different sizes piled on their straining, open arms. Edita was the only one amongst us who knew how to build a proper fire. She soon induced high flames from the crackling wood. We looked at one another quizzically when Edita doused the flames with handfuls of pine needles. Thick gray smoke began pouring from the teepee of wood, driving away the gnats and mosquitoes. I had the sudden desire to tear off my shirt and use it to send Indian smoke signals to my parents across the lake. But this would have been childish.

Edita spit the perch on the same branch she used to catch it and thrust it into the billowing smoke. She handed the branch to me, or to one of the others when she decided that more pine needles were necessary. The fire soon began to wither under the load, but right before the flames died out completely, Edita stopped adding needles and let the cone of fire rise again. She took the branch from Pawel and held the perch in the apex of the fire. Soon the skin began to split and juices danced and sizzled on the wood not yet consumed.

When the fish was cooked, we balanced steaming chunks of it on the brown bread Edita had packed in her bag and stuffed the food in our mouths quickly, so that no morsel was lost to the ground. I don't know what Aleksander and Pawel thought then, but I know, for me, that I had just eaten the best meal in the best morning of my young life.

After, the fire reduced to fading red coals, we splayed out on the flattened grass and allowed a rare hot sun to heat our already flustered faces. Edita lay inches from me. The sounds of her deepening breath formed a melody with the twittering of the birds that fed in the bushes all around us. I had the impulse to reach out and touch her arm. My cheeks burning, I clutched the grass between us. Only weeks before the very thought of touching a girl in any way had repulsed me.

...

During the afternoons we navigated the endless maze of glacial lakes and streamlets that form the Mazurian district. Edita guided our rented canoes with a knowledge that left us in awe. At least we assumed it was knowledge; maybe it was really just an instinct she had for the ways of water and wood that surpassed the book knowledge of Aleksander's mother, who taught biology in the same school where my father taught history. Our world of the ancient buildings of Torun's old town was a different universe from this realm of deer, woodchuck and heron. Wherever Edita steered us, we found a wonderland of childhood treasure: stone fire rings, some still warm and littered with broken vodka bottles, others mossed over with decades, maybe centuries, of disuse; shards of faded pottery; rusted arrow heads; discarded clothing; bullet shells; stone crosses with inscriptions too worn to read, etc. My father would have loved it, this microcosm of Polish history. But it was our world to explore; I never told him, or anyone else, about the rarest treasures we unearthed that summer.

Once we discovered a shallow grave underneath the flattened grasses where deer lay at night. The bones were less than half a meter from the surface. We were all Catholic, even Edita I supposed. The proper thing to do was to dig an appropriate grave, or even transport the bones to a consecrated churchyard. As we poked tentatively through the remains, however, we found a faded red medal with the hammer and sickle we all knew. Edita's face grew white. She scattered the bones into the forest, then drop kicked the skull into an area beneath the trees that suddenly became a makeshift pitch for a football match. We sweated away the rest of the afternoon, maneuvering the skull between our spindly legs before launching a perfect strike between the infant trees that served as goal posts. The violence of our play knocked out one tooth after another from the "ball." Eventually, Edita shattered the skull completely with one last, fearsome shot that sent a flock of crows crying from their roost.

...

Rain was ubiquitous in Mazuria that summer, as it usually is, yet the great frontal storms that produce bone-jarring thunder and crackling lightening are uncommon this far north. Instead, the clouds seep across the sky like an afterthought of God's. Sometimes they let pour their load, sometimes they didn't. One couldn't predict precipitation from the color above; almost every day the sky was a vast bowl of white with a few scraggly strips of gray thrown in for mystery. Though it rained often, it rarely did so hard enough to hamper our meanderings around the lakes. We did experience two terrific storms, however, both of which created a sulfuric smell that remains in my nose today, over twenty years later.

The first storm crept up on us while we were fast asleep. Strangely enough, it wasn't the peals of thunder that pulled me from sleep, even though once awake the noise was so loud that I felt once again enthralled by my grandfather's story about the Warsaw Uprising, indeed that I had become him, crawling through the sewers while the Hitlerites dropped grenades through the manholes.

No, it was the unmistakable song of Edita's voice. At first I thought I was dreaming. Then my body felt a warmth next to it and I realized that she lay in bed with me, talking as if I had not parted with her after dinner.

"My father isn't dead," she said.

"What?" I asked, the sleep still thick in my eyes and throat.

"He's alive," she said. "And he isn't in Siberia. He would have thrown himself into a river before being sent there. Since he's not dead, he's not there."

"Where is he?" I asked.

She let out a deep breath and slid off the bed. I felt a deep pang when she did so. I knew it was important that she remain beside me, in bed, in the dark. My mind raced. It concluded that Edita was afraid of the storm and had stolen through my window for a comfort only I could provide. Thrilled, my heart thumped with the thunder. I fumbled for my slippers and joined her at the open window. I yearned to wrap my arm around her back, but I dared not, settled instead to rest my arm against hers on the sill. We stood in silence for a moment, allowing the drops of rain blown under the eave to pelt our faces.

"Imagine a forest," she said, "the most beautiful in the world. Endless kilometers of oaks the size of giants. With birches like their wives and aspens like their children."

"And animals?" I asked.

"Yes! Everywhere you look. Hares and wild pigs and squirrels and beavers and birds of every kind."

"I like animals," I said, instantly regretting how adolescent that sounded.

"But there are no bears in this forest," Edita said.

"No bears?" I asked, trying to hide my disappointment.

"Not one. You see, there once was a whole family of bears. But long ago an army of men called the 'Forest Brothers' drove them away. My father is a Forest Brother."

"Oh," I said.

"That was a long time ago, but because my father is still there, no bears come into this forest."

"Do you ever visit your father?" I asked.

"Don't be stupid," she said, frowning at me. "Not even I know where the forest is."

I looked down at my slippers.

"Sometimes he visits me, though," she said. "And my mom, too. While we sleep."

"I like that," I said

She nodded.

"The storm is coming from the north. Let's get dressed. A bus leaves pretty soon."

"A bus?" I asked, feeling instantly sleepy again.

I should have known that this nocturnal visit had nothing to do with Edita's fear of the storm, nor even a premeditated revelation of her father's whereabouts. Her dreams were speaking to me, her words only vessels riding the currents of the storm between her unthinking mouth and my open ears. She never spoke another word about her father.

The clouds passed away, but the sky was only beginning to lighten when we gathered the rest of our party and set out for the Baltic coast, where we would find handfuls of rough amber scooped from the bottom of the sea by the storm and thrown landward. After two bus changes, we were scouring the beach. Edita could no longer surprise me with her knowledge; she knew the nature of the blue, white and orange ambers even before our frantic polishing revealed their color.

"The blue amber is the most precious we are likely to find. Black is much too rare," she said, fingering through a handful of sand and stone.

"Certain chemicals, when blended with the sap, produce the varieties you see," she continued.

By the time the last bus left for the interior, our pockets bulged with the "Baltic Gold." Over the course of the rest of the summer, we polished each minute piece we found, then painstakingly forced heated sewing needles through the stones to string them into necklaces and bracelets.

Our mothers opened the paper boxes we made containing the jewelry two days before we all left Mazuria. As we would be busy packing the next evening, that night's dinner was our last big get together with the other residents of our compound. My mother had secured a kilo of veal from a local farmer down the road and marinated the meat overnight in a bath of oil, vinegar, peppercorns and dill. Edita's mother contributed potato dumplings stuffed with pork; Aleksander's mother made three different kinds of salads; Pawel's mother strawberry compote and big bowls of blueberries with cream.

What a feast it was! We weren't accustomed to eating such a cornucopia this late in the day, if at all. By nightfall, our fathers, induced by vodka, began singing folksongs and pinching the bottoms of every woman passing their way.

Eventually, we retreated to the fire ring, and it was there that we presented our gifts to our mothers. How proud they were of our craftsmanship! And to think we had kept our little project so secret. We ceremoniously strung the necklaces on our mothers, while our fathers tipped vodka into our glasses of compote.

The rest of the evening slipped by, and I found myself shooed away to bed. I wasn't ready for sleep, even though the fire of vodka churned in my stomach for the first time, making me slightly dizzy. The adults continued their party well into the night. Before this summer, I had often sat awake in bed, listening to my parents talk behind the thin walls of our flat. No matter the hour, their talk was hushed, but I heard enough to know that they were unhappy with just about everything, including each other. On that last night of the summer of 1974, however, they boasted openly and loudly about the changes in the country. Only in the past were the days of clandestine meetings, hand delivered mimeographed copies of forbidden novels and histories, fear of secret agents. Much to my surprise, my parents often kissed openly around the fire ring that summer, and their hands were continuously entwined. Later, on the way back to Torun, they announced their attention to have another child. They were no longer afraid of bringing another life into this world, another life they'd have to feed into the Communist maw.

When my parents finally retired and began making love in the other room in our cabin as loudly as they had talked near the fire, I believed whole-heartedly that the world they were now envisioning was the real one, and that this magical summer was the first of many. There was no way for me to know that the prosperity was a shame, just smoke and mirrors, a product of hard currency loans from the West Poland would never be able to pay back. I would never have a sibling, or another summer in Mazuria, and seven years later, as I prepared for my exams to enter the University of Warsaw, my father would die in prison during the darkest days of Martial Law.

...

The second big storm arrived on the lakes our last day in the Mazurian district, though the clear sky in the morning, broken only by lines of vapor emitted by jets passing high overhead, in no way betokened the violence that would descend upon us.

As usual, Edita barged into our cabins and marched us to our waiting canoes. I had gone to bed the night before thinking I would stay behind and help my mother pack, but there was no question of defying Edita's will, or my burgeoning desire. By the time we paddled beyond sight of our cabins, the sky had darkened and a curtain of rain was clearly visible in the distance. Thunder echoed like artillery shells, and crisp lightening danced atop a stand of pine.

"We better go back," Alexander and Pawel said simultaneously.

I turned around. Both my playmates had lifted their paddles from the water and their canoe slowed to a crawl.

"Go ahead," Edita called from the front of our canoe. "We're going forward."

She looked at me and smiled.

"Yes, forward," I said, plunging my paddle back into the water.

After a moment, I heard my playmates break the distance between us. The streamlet we traveled soon narrowed. As the storm approached, closer and closer, we were forced to maneuver through the shallow water by stabbing at the encroaching banks with our paddles. By the time the streamlet opened onto a small lake, the rains came, instantly soaking us. Edita paused, pulled up her paddle and stripped off her jacket, leaving only a thin cotton blouse. The rain soon pasted the thin fabric to her back. I wiped water from my eyes and studied the contoured landscape presented to me: the hills of her shoulder blades, the subtle ridges and valleys of her ribs.

She let out a loud cackle, and then resumed her rowing with more intensity, leaving me winded and sore in my attempt to keep pace.

Once we had crossed the lake and entered another channel, the storm had abated, or at least it seemed so. Maybe I had just grown accustomed to the deluge.

"Where are we going?" Pawel shouted.

I looked around. Nothing was familiar. But how was that possible? We had conquered every square inch of those lakes, and we weren't that far from the compound. Still, not one stand of trees looked familiar, not one clearing, not one batch of lake grass.

"There!" Edita cried, pointing to somewhere ahead of us. For just a brief second, a flash passed across my eyes, as if someone a kilometer away had captured a ray of sunlight in a broken piece of mirror. There was no sun, just the thick chaos of rain and cloud, yet even today, a full generation later, that flash of light remains fixed in my mind's eye.

"Go," I shouted, paddling furiously, "go!"

In perfect tandem we ripped through the now heaving waters, across one small lake and stream after another, till we must have been long past that point Edita had found hidden in the storm. We paddled and paddled until there was no more water to traverse. We circled around a pond and only pulled our canoes ashore once we realized the only outlet was the one that had brought us that far.

"Is this it?" I asked Edita. Her front was visible to me now, the mounds of her breasts, the dark circles of her nipples face to face with my confused eyes.

She turned this way and that, bringing her finger to her puffed lips.

"Oh, yes!" she said, suddenly springing into the woods. Even though we were tired and wet, sneezing away the rain, we obediently followed, down a path she alone created. After a ten-minute futile attempt to keep up, we finally discovered Edita, in a clearing, standing face to face with, of all things, a knight in shining armor.

We three were too awestruck to say a word. We stumbled through the wet, clinging grass of the clearing until side by side with Edita.

"Impossible," I finally whispered.

Edita lifted the knight's visor and peered inside.

"A ghost-knight," she said.

"Maybe it's part of a museum," Pawel said, "or something."

"No museum," Edita replied.

"But it's brand new," Aleksander said. "No rust, or anything. What's it doing here?"

"Waiting for us?" Edita said, reaching to touch the outstretched sword. Just as her fingertip was about to make contact with the gleaming edge of the blade, a great crack of thunder shattered the air around us, followed quickly by an even more intense slap of rain. We jumped in our tracks, turned, and dove into the nearest bush. Breathing heavily, I quickly scanned the faces of my companions. Only Edita's wore no fear.

"Don't be afraid," she said. She crawled out of the bush and again headed for the knight.

"No way," Pawel said.

"I want to go home," Aleksander said, sniffling.

I peeked out of the bush and with my eyes trailed Edita's behind. One impulse froze me to the ground. Another yearned to follow. When Edita stood just a meter away from the knight, she whistled and pointed. I narrowed my eyes and peered through the rain. The knight had lowered his sword.

"She's touching the knight," I reported to Aleksander and Pawel. "Hey, she's walking by it! Let's go."

"Who cares," Pawel said. "You go, if you want."

I turned to my friends. How many summers had we passed together, kicking around a football, playing war at the garbage dump, frightening each other with ghost stories under the blankets at a sleepover? It had seemed to me that I had known them for as long as I had known my own parents. They were cold, wet, hungry, and scared. I felt disdain for them.

I looked back at the knight and said, without facing them: "I'll be back soon."

I crossed the distance to the knight. Edita was nowhere in sight. I paused at the miraculous suit of metal, waiting for a breath, anticipating the sword rising for a strike. When nothing happened, I tapped the breastplate. The armor remained immobile. I continued walking, through a narrow path in the woods behind the knight. Within a few steps the opening in the trees began to narrow. When I thought I could go no further, I heard Edita call from behind a curtain of blackness.

"Come on!"

Only then did I discover that the path led to a small hole in a hillock. I dropped to my knees. Sure enough, a bright light pierced the dark. I crawled, small stones and branches biting my palms and knees. The rain no longer blanketed my body, now only the absence of color, save the arch of light in front of me. I fought through the shadows, shimmying across the ground, reaching for the light. Just as the cave became too small for my body, its stone sides scraping holes into my jacket, was I through, standing up, face to face with Edita.

"Isn't it wondrous?" she said, spreading her arms.

My jaw dropped.

Illuminated by hidden lights, a room of amber.

A dining set: knives, forks, spoons, plates, and bowls carved from hunks of white amber, swirled with black. The table, the chairs, of equally white amber placed majestically below a chandelier dripping with raindrops of golden amber. The walls, the ceiling, panels of amber. Then there were chess sets, and champagne glasses, cruets, wine bottles, serving trays. A desk, a set of pens, books with covers of amber. Along another wall a complete bed: a mattress of blue amber, a pillow of black amber, and a blanket of cards of equally black amber knitted together with gold wire. A doll of gold amber with clothes of silk. Beside the bed, two imposing thrones, carved into their amber backs and armrests, dragons and knights and crowns and ladies-in-waiting.

We laughed, for what else could we do? We laughed like only children can laugh, till our sides hurt, a celebration of life, of youth, of hope. We laughed until we could no more, and then, I reached for Edita, taking her arms in my hands, and kissed her on the lips. Our eyes remained open wide. It surprised both of us. After, Edita swirled away, the rainwater still dripping from her trousers onto the amber floor. She skipped across the room, giggling, and then bounced down into a throne.

"Now I will be your queen," she said.

I crossed the room and eased into the throne next to her, gingerly running my fingers across the carved armrests. I studied the opulence all around me, this vast spread of wealth more than anything I could have imagined before, and grinned at the recollection of the silly little amber trinkets that had so pleased our mothers. I dropped my hand onto Edita's and looked into her eyes where a hidden fire danced and spread its wings.

Oh how that fire burns me still, twenty years past. If only I had tapped the magic of those three months in Mazuria, had captured Edita and this room of amber in a sphere less fragile than a waking dream. Perhaps my life would have been a better one.

"And I will be your king," I said.

SHALLOW GRAVE

On the third day of the siege of Przemysl Wojtek had been so drunk by the heat of battle that he did not feel the three shards of shrapnel pierce his left thigh. Not until he leaned against the breastworks, drinking homemade vodka with what remained of his Polish regiment, did he notice his torn leggings and the blood darkening the field of blue and knew that it was time to scream in pain. Before he could ask his comrades to help him to the field hospital, the Madonna whispered in his ear that he should not go, that his duty was to help bury the fallen. He wrapped his thigh with the white blouse his wife had sewn him and the next morning continued to fire his rifle alongside the Czechs, Hungarians and the other Poles who formed the front line of the Austrian army. Before the full heat of the day had parched Wojtek's throat, a Russian artillery shell destroyed the hospital.

After the war ended Wojtek walked two months back to his family farm near Grodno, his hands permanently calloused by the many graves he had dug. Whether or not the Madonna saw fit to warn his wife and child of the danger in their future he never knew. By the time he reached home, they had been taken away by the influenza ravaging the countryside. The bodies, dwindled by two months of decomposition, were in a tight embrace on the bed which had carried the weight of both mother's and child's conception and birth. In death, Wojtek's wife and son lay lightly on the goose feather mattress. When he lifted the skin and bones from their resting place, the feathers did not rise with the alleviation of their burden. As he carried away the remains, Wojtek wondered if they really were the earthly remnants of his loved ones, or if they were their spirits, as light as a loose bundle of hay.

His family gone, he worked his farm alone. During the first plowing season, two of the pieces of shrapnel worked their way to the surface of his skin and dropped into the furrows of the field. The wheat that came from the field grew taller and fuller than in any years previous and he quickly became one of the wealthiest farmers in the region. The third piece of shrapnel did not make its way to the surface; it burrowed deeper into his thigh until it brushed against bone. He felt it most when the rains came and only then did he know real pain. He developed the limping gait that would hound him for the rest of his life.

As they had so many times before, the Russians invaded Poland in 1920. Wojtek dug a tunnel under his property and buried his earthly possessions. Only his Austrian rifle, which he cleaned and oiled, did he keep aboveground. When Marshal Pilsudski called for volunteers to recoil the Russian advance, Wojtek, despite his wound, answered without hesitation. He was present at the "Miracle of the Vistula" and was told by the great marshal himself that the Polish Eagle inhabited his body and gave him the surest, deadliest aim in the army. The Poles pushed back the Russians into the steppes of Belarus, and after the General reclaimed Wilno for Poland, Wojtek danced a waltz with a wealthy Jewess, despite his bad leg, in a cafe in the center of the city. Thus began a month-long affair that brought a happiness Wojtek would never know again. One night, as he walked the Jewess home after a symphony concert, a band of Lithuanian Nationalists jumped out of an alley and sent a barrage of bullets from handmade pistols into the unsuspecting, happy couple. Wojtek escaped with a flesh wound to his shoulder. The Jewess had taken the brunt of the attack. Her body riddled with bullets, Wojtek carried her home, despite the blood seeping from his own body, and laid her on the bed which had once brought them only joy. He held her through the night, and just before dawn broke, the Madonna whispered in his ear that it was time to go home. He opened his eyes and realized that the Jewess was dead. He wrapped her in fresh linen and buried her in the flowerbed she had been caring for since the death of her parents.

Before leaving Wilno, Wojtek revisited the sight of the attack. Wedged in the brickwork of a bakery was the bullet that had passed through his right shoulder. He pried it out with his knife and dropped it into his pocket before heading back to his farm.

Three months later, he sold his silverware, which had been in his family since before the Partitions, for two cows and thirty chickens. He took the Lithuanian bullet out of his pocket and tossed it into the center of the pond where the cows and chickens would water. The fields had been dormant during his absence. He worked the fields night and day and planted them with the seeds he had hidden. The wheat once again thrived. The two cows calved that first season, even though they had not been mated. The chickens laid more eggs than any others in the region, and Wojtek once again became wealthy.

His wounds, however, made him lamer with each passing year. Soon he was not able to plough his extensive farm. Wojtek did not need all his land; he now had more money than he ever thought he could spend. He was not a vain man, either. He did not build a mansion in place of the two-room wooden home he was accustomed to, nor did he buy one of the fancy motor cars all the rage in newly independent Poland. He made do with a team of horses and simple carriage, and donated large portions of his wealth to the Church. The rest he converted into gold coin and stockpiled in the tunnel beneath his property.

Wojtek began leasing out parcels of his land to men in the village. However, these fields proved to be far less bountiful than the one Wojtek continued to work. The grace bestowed to him was not transferred to farmers working a few meters away. He was labeled a witch. The men in the village no longer drank with him, and their children threw stones at the storks nesting on his rooftop. One boy, who grew up on the first parcel of land Wojtek had leased, heaved a large rock through his living room window one night, which struck Wojtek in the temple as he sat reading a newspaper. For years the boy was merciless. He stole eggs from the hen house and beat one of the cows with a log. He did not care if Wojtek knew he was the culprit. Wojtek never tried to prove it. The boy looked like his own son, the boy who had died of influenza, or at least he could have looked like him, had Wojtek's son survived.

Wojtek watched the boy turn into a young man. He saw him accept his First Communion, and then his Confirmation. He witnessed his first fight, ached for him as his nose was bloodied and he was beaten to the ground. Six months later, Wojtek beamed when the boy broke the jaw of the one who had so easily dispatched him before. Wojtek's heart beat fast when the boy kissed his first girl on the side of his outhouse. First, memories of the Jewess, the last woman Wojtek had touched, coursed through his mind's eye, then there was his wife, whom he could no longer easily remember, standing in front of him in bridal white, as clearly as she did so many years earlier. It wasn't until then that Wojtek discovered loneliness. He found comfort only in the fact that the Madonna still whispered into his ear late at night.

The boy stopped stealing, but Wojtek began leaving eggs and trussed chickens on the family's doorstep.

The boy, now sixteen, had grown stout and hard from his work in the fields. Wojtek had grown weaker and knew that his days as a farmer were numbered. When the Hitlerites and the Russians invaded Poland in September, the boy prepared to leave the village with the others too young to fight in the regular army. Wojtek once again oiled his rifle and hobbled into the town square to join them.

When the boys saw the lame Wojtek, dressed in his carefully mended uniform from the Great War, they heckled and jeered.

"Ah, it's the witch!"

"Fly away on your broom, old woman!"

"Go milk your cow!"

"Old man," the boy said, thrusting his face into Wojtek's, "your time is over."

He tore the rifle out of the old man's hands and shoved him to the ground.

"This, we can use," the boy said, setting the rifle against his shoulder.

Wojtek remained on the ground as the small band of boys marched out of town and headed for the vast primeval forest to the south.

"Holy Mother, protect them," he said.

...

When the Russians arrived a week later, they found only one cow and a few scrawny chickens on Wojtek's farm. He had slaughtered and salted the rest of his stock and buried it in his tunnel. His wheat and corn had not yet matured. The Russians took what was edible and burned the rest. When the soldiers saw how decrepit Wojtek was, they only kicked and punched him, instead of impressing him into their army.

In March, when the ground was still hard from the winter, the Madonna told him to plant his crops. He labored day and night, without the use of his horse, which had been taken away by the Russians before Christmas. The ground was unmerciful, but Wojtek managed to plow it, and when the Russians came at harvest to claim their share, his wheat was already baked into the hardtack that lay hidden in his tunnel.

"The partisans took it," he said. "I have only this." He produced two bottles of vodka from beneath his straw mattress.

The Russians laughed. When they saw how scrawny the old man was, they doubted whether he was able to plant anything at all. They beat him and kicked him once again, then took the vodka, believing that the old man would never live to see another harvest.

Throughout the time of the Russian occupation, Wojtek continued to leave offerings of food for the boy, as well as his comrades. He wrapped salted meat and hardtack into old newspaper and placed it on the boy's old doorstep under the cover of darkness. The boy's mother and only surviving sister, both of whom had become mute and deaf after repeated rapes, took a small share, but Wojtek knew that most of it went to the partisans fighting the Russians in the forest.

The Russians departed as abruptly as they arrived. When the Hitlerites knocked down Wojtek's door, he was standing at attention in his old uniform. The soldiers laughed. Two of them sat down at Wojtek's table and lit cigarettes. The third left on an errand, but he soon returned with a colonel. The two soldiers who had stayed behind leapt to attention. The colonel mentioned them to go, but before they did so, they dropped a leaflet with the rules of the occupation in Polish. From the moment the Hitlerites entered, Wojtek remained standing, at attention.

The colonel lit a cigarette. He was gray around the temples and had a slight paunch to this stomach. He studied Wojtek for a moment, then took off his glasses and rubbed his eyes.

"Sit," he said.

Wojtek hesitated for a moment before hobbling to the table.

"Where did you get the limp?" he asked, in German.

"Przemsyl, sir."

"Of course. The Austrians. Cowards, most of them. Almost as bad as you Poles."

"I shot my share of Russians, sir."

"Of course. Haven't we all?"

Wojtek remained quiet.

"Still, you Poles are a peculiar race. Famous for fighting lost causes. This war is over for you. For all Poles. Remember this." The colonel picked up the leaflet and dropped it on the table in front of Wojtek.

"We fought a common enemy in the last war," he continued. "We will continue to do so, whether that enemy be Russian, Jew, or Pole."

It was a statement, not a question. Wojtek obediently answered:

"Yes, sir."

"Maybe you heard five shots coming from the square," the colonel said. "One of my men was killed by a partisan today. Five Poles paid for it. Next time it will be ten. A tiresome business. It is only a matter of time before we round up the rest of the partisans. You have the largest farm in this area. You know everyone, everyone knows you. You will help us, in any way possible."

"Yes, sir."

Before the colonel left he took one last look at the mended trousers of Wojtek's uniform, then dropped a packet of Turkish cigarettes on the table. The three soldiers stormed back into the house and ransacked it. They found only a half loaf of baker's bread, a small piece of salt pork and a bulging sack of raw wheat. The concealed entrance to the tunnel below eluded them. Not until they were long gone and the chirping of crickets filled the night did Wojtek push back the table and climb down into his tunnel. Now, his most prized possession was the small, hand-cranked mill he used to grind the kernels of wheat into flour. This one simple tool could bring a death sentence, since all farmers were now required to take their wheat to the central mill, which was supervised by a Hitlerite.

Wojtek ground enough wheat to fill a large sack of hardtack. There was a new moon outside, and thick cloud cover to douse the smoke coming from the chimney, so he took the chance that the soldiers would not return that night and built the small fire required to bake the bread. When dawn began to tease the horizon with its pink wash, he filled a sack with hardtack, strips of jerky and gold coin. He closed the sack with thin wire and carried it to the outhouse. Two nights earlier he had covered the waste at the bottom of the outhouse with sand and lime. Since then, he had been defecating in a bucket and burying the waste inside the abandoned chicken coop. Under the rim of the wooden frame of the toilet he nailed the loose end of the wire, and let the sack of food hang suspended inches above the sand and lime. The hole was deep and dark enough that the burlap and wire could not be seen.

When the sun was above the horizon, he obediently hefted a sack of wheat and carried it to the mill. Soldiers confiscated three quarters of the flour he had ground. The boy's mother and sister were there, as were most of the farmers. Wojtek slipped a note into the mother's hand, with the words "First Kiss" scrawled in pencil.

Months passed. The merchant Jews who owned and worked the fine stores around the central square were taken away. Occasionally shots could be heard in the forest, or loud explosions. After each disturbance, villagers were lined up and shot. Soon only old men like Wojtek, women and children were left in Grodno.

He continued to leave the burlap sacks in the outhouse. Sometimes it would be weeks before the food was taken. At night he wondered if he should continue supporting the partisans at all. So many people were dying, indirectly, from their actions. Every time he convinced himself to stop leaving the food, the Madonna whispered in his ear and told him to suspend even more sacks above the waste in the outhouse.

When the Hitlerites first arrived in Grodno, they charged through the countryside like avenging angels. The butts of their rifles shone like swords in the summer sun, and their tanks gleamed and screeched like the horses of the Apocolypse. During their advance not even the Madonna showed her majesty in Wojtek's lonely room, and only rarely, during the occupation, did he feel her presence, when the nights were quiet as the bottom of the sea, and his mind was settled enough to feel her cool breath caress his cheek. On the return of the now retreating army, three harvests after their advance, the Hitlerites' manhood was revealed through their tattered clothing, their stumbling gait, and the fear in their eyes, which frightened the storks from Wojtek's rooftop.

Soon, he knew, the Russians would return, and the provisional government of the Hitlerites would fall. Maybe, Wojtek hoped, the boy had survived these five years. Somehow. And if he were alive, Wojtek would take him as far from this place as he possibly could. To America, even.

Such dreams, however, were not his to fulfill. The colonel visited Wojtek one last time before he took what occupation troops he had back to Berlin for their final stand. He kicked open the door, and again, Wojtek greeted him in his uniform, at attention.

This time, it was the colonel who shouted in laughter. The two boy soldiers at his side, who couldn't have been older than sixteen, remained as stone-faced and frightened as Wojtek's companions in the Great War.

"The war might be over," the colonel said, "but there are still enemies to dispatch." He produced a shovel from outside the door and threw it into Wojtek's arms.

"Come."

Wojtek followed the Hitlerites, through the breadth of his lands and into the dark forest. The only light to guide them through the maze of oaks came from the whites of the four pairs of eyes and the dim electric torch of the colonel. Like his Savior before him, Wojtek fell three times en route. The first time a root caught his foot, the second time, he felt a hand shove him from behind, but when he looked back, the two frightened soldiers were still five paces away. The third time he dropped from exhaustion. The colonel pulled him up roughly by the collar and pushed him forward. When they reached a small opening in the woods, the colonel stopped.

"Dig," he said.

The grass, straight and stiff, scratched Wojtek's sore legs. He knew this place. As a child, he often woke before the sun and made the trek into the forest to try to startle the bison that slept here. No matter how early he arrived, however, he always missed them. The only memory they left behind was the flattened grass of their beds and the musky smell of their sudden departure.

"Dig."

The bison were long gone. There was no use to wait for them. But where was the Madonna in these moments before his death?

"Why have you forsaken me?" he cried out.

Thunder rumbled in the distance. He looked up to the sky but found only stars. He had no answer from God, only the advancing Russian artillery.

"Dig, damn you!" The colonel slapped him in the face, hard enough to knock down Wojtek, but he stood his ground and took in the hot, stagnant breath of the Hitlerite.

"Dig," the colonel repeated, quietly.

Wojtek drove the blade of the shovel through the thick roots of the grass. As soon as the blade found dirt, adrenaline surged through his body and blanketed any pain he felt from his old wounds. He had dug so many graves in his life. He knew he had strength for his own. As he ripped through the grass and threw aside large clods of dirt and clay, the colonel stepped aside and lit a cigarette. The rumble of the artillery continued. The colonel took long, slow drags. Wojtek heaved and sweated through his task and did not slow when he felt the blood seep up to the surface from his wounds. When the two faces of the women in his mortal life appeared in the deepening hole, he did not stop to admire their beauty, or to remember how he felt in their arms, but dug faster until he uncovered the face of his boy, and the faces of his parents, and siblings, and grandparents, and the faces of all he had once knew, now dead to this earth and living in the glory of God.

"Enough, old man," he heard the colonel say. "How much ground is one dirty Pole worth?" Before Wojtek could drive in the shovel once more, the colonel grabbed it from his bleeding hands and pulled him from the grave.

"Now, stand at attention."

In the last of his strength, Wojtek stood tall on the lip of the grave and faced the boy soldiers who jammed bullets into the chambers of their rifles.

"Mother of God forgive me," he said. "Accept me into your arms."

The colonel chuckled, pitching aside a burning cigarette, which, after reaching the zenith of its arch, descended into the shallow grave.

The shallowness of the grave reminded Wojtek of the shallowness of his life. He had lived so many years already, but now those years felt like only a brief, pleasant dream fighting for desperate breath amongst uncountable nightmares of war and death.

Now the Madonna made her return. Her fingertips felt like cool drops of rain on his forehead and stiffening shoulders.

"Do not be afraid," she whispered.

The colonel whistled. Wojtek heard a shout, steel hitting steel, the grass under the trees scuffling against boots.

"Step aside, old man," the colonel said. "This one's not for you."

Into the clearing shot beams of electric torches, followed by helmeted soldiers. Between them stumbled the boy, hands bound behind his back. Five years older, his face bloodied and bruised, his body clothed in the same garments in which he left Grodno five years earlier. Now those clothes hung in tatters on his emaciated frame. He looked at Wojtek then, but in his last merciful gesture, he failed to recognize him. The boy walked on his own power to the lip of the grave.

"Go ahead, you Nazi bastards," he croaked out between broken teeth.

...

When it was over, the Hitlerites turned without a word and seeped into the trees, leaving Wojtek alone to bury the boy. He had every intention of pulling the boy out of the grave to dig to a more appropriate depth, but he saw then that the Madonna had done the work for him. The boy was at peace now. Wojtek took the remainder of the night to fill the grave and to fashion a cross from fallen oak limbs. As he worked, it crossed his mind, so briefly, that he should have somehow taken the boy's place. But that was impossible. It was his fate to live, to walk this earth long enough to bury all whom he would ever love, and it was always this way.

RED, UNDER THE TREES

I.

On the eve of Jagienka's Name Day, her mother coaxed her into a trunk and blanketed her with clothes still pungent with freshly furrowed fields. The girl thought it a game, pushed her five-year-old body through her father's stockings, trousers and shirts as if she were swimming through the river bordering the family's estate. When the cool amber buttons brushed her cheeks, she imagined that the fishes kissed her, wishing her one hundred years of health and happiness with each peck.

"My little fishes," she whispered. "I will share my cake with you tomorrow."

"Please, my little mushroom," her mother said sternly. "Not a word. Not a sound until I let you out. Or there will be no cake tomorrow."

And because Jagienka could already taste the thick, sugary icing and the filling of apples and cinnamon, she made no sound at all, even when the neighing horses clattered onto the cobblestoned porch and men shouting in a language only vaguely familiar burst into the manor house.

"Please," her mother urged as she turned the key in the trunk, "not a word."

The key was removed. Jagienka pressed her eye to the keyhole and watched her mother's long silk gown retreat towards the door. Her mother looked back then and placed a finger on her lips, reminding her to remain silent. The keyhole, with its rounded top and triangular bottom, framed her mother's shape perfectly. Jagienka wondered if her father had returned a day early, and if all the disturbance outside was nothing but town men bringing in what must be the biggest of all presents. She giggled to herself and dove back into the river of clothes.

When her mother reentered the room, Jagienka once again pressed her eyes to the keyhole. There was a flurry of activity. Sharp images she'd remember the rest of her life drilled into her mind: the glint of a saber, three pairs of boots, brown stems of grass pressed into caked mud, red blotches. She caught an odor too, of the type the servants wore before the "Troubles" sent them away. Her heart skipped a beat, for she missed the kindly old woman that used to bath her and cook her morning kasha.

"Please, no," her mother said, in a voice too quiet for her, as if she were a small animal, Jagienka thought, like the wild hare her father shot in the woods.

A slap. A muffled cry. Clothing ripped. One pair of boots swung over the chest and a great weight made the hinges groan. Now she looked between a man's legs, worried that the chest would shatter from the load on top of it. Still, she remained silent, just as her mother had instructed. But what of her father? His smell wasn't here, just that of the men who worked in the field, or the Jews, or the shop girls who sat in the common pews at Mass.

The laced dress. The muddy boots. The legs of her parents' bed and the bleached down comforter.

"There's another room," her mother said, once again in the voice of the hare. "It's much nicer."

A man spat some words. Another slap. Her mother tumbled onto the edge of the bed. She looked as if she were about to slide off when a pair of arms, sleeved in dirty blue wool and topped with tarnished gold epaulets, thrust into Jagienka's field of vision and grabbed her mother's bottom and pushed it up, till it teetered on the edge. With her mother's back flat on the bed, the arms went to work on the linen and lace underneath the inverted cone of her dress, tearing with grimy fingers and slicing with a keen-edged knife. The smudged petticoats collected at the man's boots like dirty, late winter snow.

Now those fumbling fingers were untying his trousers, and these soon too collected at the boots. Jagienka saw her mother's bare legs; they were enveloped with fine golden down that sparkled in the sunlight. The man's legs were covered in harsh black hairs. Jagienka's gaze traveled up those legs and stopped. Was that a third arm? The connection was hazy, but she now understood why her mother warned her away from the swineherd as if he were the devil himself.

With his two larger arms, the man once again bent down, this time roughly pulling at her mother's legs. She gasped and said "no" yet again. The man lifted her legs and pushed them towards her head. Her mother's neck arched and reddened, as if a stone was trying to force itself from her throat. Now, with her legs on either side of her body and against the mattress, the man's forearm pressing them taut, her mother looked as if she had been cut in half. Jagienka choked back a gasp. As much as she wanted to look away, she felt as if she couldn't even blink.

The boots shuffled. The pile of linen and lace fluttered. The man's third arm disappeared inside of her mother. Her head lifted from the mattress and turned towards the chest. For one brief second, Jagienka caught her eye. But then her mother turned her head away, and while she wanted more than anything to call out to her, Jagienka doubted, even if she did, that she'd be heard, for the man on top of her mother had what sounded like a coughing fit, but a long one, so long that the man sitting on the chest began pounding his boots into the floorboards in unison. Soon followed a clapping from the other side of the room, feebly attempting to hold the rhythm.

The man sputtered one last cough before pulling away from her mother and dripping from his third arm to the petticoats on the floorboards. He mumbled something, pulled up his trousers and bowed deeply so the sword tied to his waist sprang up behind his back and caught the sunlight rippling through the window, illuminating it like an angel's wing. He even flourished a make-believe hat, just as the man guests did when they partook of the Christmas dinner.

The chest squeaked and groaned once again. The feet, all by themselves, it seemed, walked over to her mother, still in half on the bed, even though the first man no longer held her legs to her sides. This second man stopped in front of her and dropped his trousers just like the first. Initially Jagienka couldn't see a third arm because of this man's meatier thighs. But then he reached down between them, and soon there was the third arm. His hand moved on it, as if greeting a timber cutter in the square. Like his thighs, his third arm was thicker and longer than the first man's. There was a sharp intake of breath, and then one of the men laughed. When this third arm went into her mother, Jagienka's throat dried up. The man began to move and make his noises. Jagienka's mouth opened and closed, as if she really were swimming in the depths of the river, taking in the water to quench her thirst. She closed her eyes and tried to quietly sink deeper into the chest, but like a fallen branch she couldn't help but break the surface of clothes and reach for the light of the keyhole, her eye sifting through the tumbling dust motes, back to the scene on the bed.

When this man finished, he did not gallantly bow or reach for a make-believe hat. As her mother whimpered, Jagienka could now hear, the man wiped his third arm with his hand and flung something red and yellowish, like some awful kind of thick broth, onto the white petticoats.

"Polish whore!" he shouted. And this Jagienka could understand.

Moments later, the man resumed his place, the chest suffering under his bulk.

Laughter, once again. Another pair of boots, though these shuffled, in short, hesitant slides, across the floor. The last came completely into view only after he placed himself in front of her mother and drooped forward to loosen his baggy trousers. His face flashed in Jagienka's vision. He was clearly younger than the other two, no more than a boy really, just as young as the baker's son who delivered the daily bread. His thighs were thin, white and hairless. He said something to her mother in a quiet voice that made the other men shout what could only be insults. The boy hurled back some words, his voice cracking, and he immediately tried to shake his third arm. Whatever worked for the last man didn't work for the boy. He tugged and tugged, but nothing grew. He switched to his other hand, and when that didn't do it, he stamped his foot and swung it at the bed, his trousers tripping him up and landing him onto the woman. Now Jagienka saw his bright red cheeks sliced with trails of tears as he spat on her mother and beat her with his small fists.

Of all that she had witnessed, this Jagienka thought, at her tender age, to be the worst her mother endured: this boy who was barely grown, this Not Yet Man, swinging at her mother because he wasn't at all like his two friends. Even they, perhaps, were disturbed by his outburst. The heavy man lifted himself from the chest. The other, the first, sprang back into the view, pulled the boy from the bed and threw him to the ground, first shouting, then laughing, but no longer allowing him to touch her mother.

After a few moments, the voices, the laughter, grew dim. The men shambled about the room, picking up bits that had fallen from their pockets, stomping their boots once again, loosening dried mud that spattered to the floorboards like animal droppings. Her mother, still whimpering oh so quietly, unfolded herself, straightening her body so her head reached where the pillows should be, but now, because of the angle, Jagienka could only see her trembling legs and the thick pyramid of hair ending at the top.

The boots. The legs. The glinting saber seemed no longer concerned with what lay on the bed. The men retreated, marching through the hall and down the stairs. Things crashed to the floor as they went. Jagienka imagined vases in pieces, paintings torn from their mountings, her father's brass bugle clattering to the floor. The sounds grew more distant, and still her mother didn't move from the bed, and Jagienka did not call out. The men got to what must have been the crockery, but perhaps only a few pieces hit the floor. The noises soon faded. The men might have been bored, or tired, or been called away.

Like the men, Jagienka too faded, into the blackness of night. Before she went under, images replayed in her mind: the glint of steel, the buffed, black leather, the sobs of her broken mother. Soon though, something clicked, buried below her consciousness. The images went the way of smoke and then she dreamt of her birthday cake, and sharing it with her fish friends, before she was scooped out of the river with a soft net, a familiar smell, and carried back to her very own bed.

II.

On the first day, I bathe the girl. My legs still sore from the carriage ride. Three days from Kaunas. I bend and scrub this girl. I look and feel for the Mark. For the horn growth. Or tail. When there's nothing, I say the bed bugs avoid her. Not even fleas she's so fresh and pretty.

"You talk funny," she says. "Are you from France?"

"Don't be stupid."

"Father said I was to get a French tutor. All the best ladies in Warsaw have them. And an Austrian seamstress..."

"Quit your wriggling. Or I'll smack you one."

"And a Georgian cook. A Venetian to teach me the voice."

"You got me instead."

"Why?"

"No one wants to come."

"I don't understand."

"Lift your feet. For the love of all that's holy."

"Why won't they come? Father said...."

"'Father said, Father said.' Yes, yes, but they're not coming. You see?"

"Why?"

"Your god forsook this country, that's why."

"My god?"

"The Czar."

"We don't say such things in this house."

Fine. Then give me a blessed few moments of silence. I lift her out and towel her.

"Will you teach me to dance? To sing? To embroider?"

"No. Move your arms."

"What then?"

"To wipe your own arse."

...

This girl, she's okay. Maybe not so bright but curious. She's pale white, given her class. Not plump, but strong. She won't be buried anytime soon. Unless she has to care for herself. Then by the Holiest, she'd have coin on her eyes.

But the mother? Ach. It's good her daughter is strong. She won't be having another. Despite she's of the church and her god tells her to. She's nothing short of a spirit walking these rooms. A siren without the song. Or at least she sings so softly her husband doesn't hear now. He doesn't visit her bed, I think, not even when the moon is right. I change the linen. But why bother? There's no night sweat, or spilled seed. In the square, the chicken hawker tells me, "Last year, she got her share and got it good."

Like so many noble women. On estates all over, even in Lithuania. That was the Czar's warning. Don't keep up with this funny business.

This is the way of things now. Even the Nobles aren't safe. A Lady. A rag picker. A cunt's a cunt.

And now? A year ago, that was. This mother, her breasts still high, supple thighs. She sits there in her fancy dresses. At the mini piano, the for-tay. Her hair like fine threads of linen. Here but not here. Dressed, but nothing breathing inside. She raises her fingers above the keys. Then? She stares at the wall, but there's nothing there to see. Her hands stay there, above the keys, until they tremble. I grab them and push them to her sides. Her skin so soft, so smooth. This mother, she smells of youth.

I curse her for the waste.

...

The husband (the *Master*), he gives me the rubles for the household. The priest comes for the child's catechism. I give him some rubles because I'm told to. Then here's the seamstress for the spring measurements. She gets a few. Even though I can sew. The knife sharpener. The hog butcher. The cobbler. The tuner? Not a copeck. Staring at the for-tay doesn't break it. The baker boy nearly gets my foot in his backside. I can make bread as any. I try and give some rubles back, but the *Master*, he just stares at them, like it's a female thing he can't swallow. I take what's left and bury it in the hay. I keep doing it.

...

I bake two loaves, brown, heavy as stone. Thick enough to get the wolf through the Siberian winter. One loaf, I bury in the fields, pour ale over the mound. To the Earth I give. As it gives to me. I keep doing this.

At table, there's the other loaf. The family, the three, they stare at it.

"The boy did not deliver?" the *Master*, he asks. Not looking at me. Not even talking to me. Or anyone. "I will talk with his keeper."

The girl, she takes a bite too small for a mouse even. Then she spits it out. I slap the back of her head. Not hard. Just enough to make her know. That's food. The *Master*, he stands, the glasses rattling. The mother? No move. Just taps her cabbage soup with her spoon. I thought the girl would wail, this one. But no. She looks at me.

"We are accustomed to the white bread," the man says. "You need not strike the child."

"The white gives you bad air."

This shocks him, the *Master*, no end. His eyes go way up. The girl, she just looks and looks, like a baby bird waiting for its worm. The mother? She's leagues away.

"Nevertheless, that is what we eat ... have eaten."

I go to take away the bread. Before though, the girl, she pops the crumb back into her mouth. Then, she tears into the slice. Eats the soup.

"Very well, then." The *Master*.

And after. For many suppers, I serve the cutlet, potato, the *cepelinai*, the stuffed pike. The Lithuanian way. The girl, she prods and pokes. Then I shuffle behind her, maybe, till she tries it. The *Master*, he doesn't eat, or like to eat, not until the girl, she has some. She eats. He eats. The wife? Maybe she eats.

Sometimes, he looks at her funny, the girl. For no reason, he stops and grabs her. Squeezes her tight till her eyes bug out. Then, the *Master*, he goes on about the French tutor and Austrian seamstress.

"Someday soon, my child, they will come."

He says this. Over and over. Why? Maybe a devil knows. I was called to protect her, this girl, this orphan. No one else will come soon. Least not from foreign lands. The old *Master*, this one's cousin, he was glad to be rid of me I think.

When the First Communion dress comes, the *Master*, he sends it back. Not once. Not twice. Eight times. He stoops low and gets a Jew to make it finally.

Was he the *Master*? Or the girl?

I tell the peasant at the coop: "A rooster comes into the house? I ring your neck and stew *you*."

There's no dragon sign outside. Inside? I prod the girl's clothes for snake. Nothing. For good measure, I prod his, the *Master's*. Nothing. I keep doing this. Nothing, over and over.

Their souls are still their own.

...

The *Master*, he buys the girl dolls. Too many to count. She has a room to herself, this girl. That's bad enough. It fills with dolls, with porcelain faces and porcelain hands. Not even for Christmas or Name Days, but with every package from Warsaw.

Still, the *Master*, he squeezes her to red face. For no reason. The Nobles, they don't do such things. Sometimes, I wake before the rooster and the girl, she's curled next to me in the attic. Men are funny, but the *Master*, he seems good for a Catholic. Still, there are man-needs. The wife, she is no wife. So I squeeze the milt from the herring, cover the pickled roe with it. No matter what, the wife, she gets this. In her cabbage, in her dumpling. All the days leading up to the moon-call. Then, I sneak down from the attic and listen for the sounds of marriage.

The *Master's* room? Only snoring. Hers? Not a peep. I pinch off the flame and open the door. Blue in the moonlight, the mother, she's on her back, arms crossed on her flat stomach. Like stone, like an Old One frozen in their cathedral. I close her nose. Wait. Not so long and she gasps. But small, like a kitten. Opens her eyes.

"Sleep."

She does. Not even Love Apple would heat her blood.

After the morning kasha, the constable, he and I talk at the station. Then I sweep and soap and scrub the out-building near the chickens. I fill it with the finest furniture, the mattress with the softest down. The windows? I darken with charcoal. The cow woman, she glares with hatred, what, the straw she sleeps on.

"For an egg girl?" She spits.

"The *Master*, he likes his eggs."

She comes, the egg girl. Black hair, brown eyes. High breast, long fingers. She's Tartar. Dressed like a peasant, but moves like what she is. The rubles I bury in the hay are more than enough for her. The *Master*, he doesn't take long to sniff her out, like a fox to a ground nest.

When her blood flows, the Tartar, I push aside the dolls and sleep at the girl's foot. The other days? When the scent of the Tartar's flesh calls for him? In my mind, the *Master*, he laps at her. As the sea to the sand. Before the pull of the moon is so great that he crashes into her. Drops of their lust like perfect pebbles of amber on the beach.

I curse them their love.

...

I bathe her, the girl. Her white skin turns red.

"Where are your mother and father?" she asks.

"Dead."

"Where is your husband?"

"Dead."

She tries to taste the lye.

"Don't be stupid." I grab her wrist.

"Did you love him?"

"Who taught you such nonsense? Love."

"Where are your children?"

"Dead."

The girl, she looks at me.

"Did you love them?"

Love? Six, I had. All pulled dead from me, disfigured and black, like potatoes with the blight. The first? The midwife, she vomited at the sight. Crossed herself. Prayed to her god. The second? She was more prepared, took it away before I could look. The same with the third. The fourth. The fifth. The sixth. In the birthing bed, there was so much pain my toes gnarled, turned into feet like an eagle's. Still the shoes hurt me.

Did I love my babies? Spawns of a devil, they said. Maybe. But their spirits, they stretch in the limbs of the oak, the ash, the birch. Their hearts, they beat in the earth. In the fields I walk and feel their blood pushing at my feet. Now, as ever. Like the willow I weep. The ground pulling down my branches. I won't be whole until they're once again roots in the ground, holding the spawn to my breast.

Did I love them?

"Don't be stupid."

...

The rains come. Then the sun. Then the dying off. The snows. Over and again. The girl, she grows long and limber. Soon she will bear the fruit. The *Master*, he's a man. The Tartar? She must stay young. But she wants the Condition. A son for her Master. Like a hare to a vegetable patch she eyes the estate. I crush the seeds of wild carrot into powder, sprinkle it in her morning kasha to dry out the womb. I use her greed to keep her wet, keep her wanting.

...

The girl, she's old enough to bathe herself. I heat and haul the water and prepare her brushes and soaps. Guard the kitchen door. She wants none of that.

"I'm lonely," she calls.

So I bend and scrub.

"Soon my father will be taking me to Warsaw to meet Society. Oh, there will be dancing and cakes and wines and, and boys!"

She hits the water. Gets it in my eye.

"Stop your foolishness."

"You must come, Laume. I don't think Mother will."

"Your mother won't."

Her chest, the girl's, it's still flat. But her blond locks bounce from her shoulders when she walks. Maybe like the mother once. And she has the fairness about her cheeks, but no breasts?

"Will I meet my husband there?"

No breasts. The father, his estate about as plump. Good enough for the Tartar whore. But a young bull from Warsaw?

"Perhaps, Child. Perhaps."

"Is that how you met yours?"

"Ach, your questions!"

"You had lovers first?" In a whisper.

"I'm old."

The girl, she looks at me with big eyes. Like always. Since I first came.

I'm old. Old enough to remember the column of beautiful French soldiers marching through the streets of Kaunas. Their fresh uniforms. Their shiny swords.

"Impale me!" I want to yell.

How I swoon. How I fall in love with dozens, maybe hundreds of them.

My neighbors, they cry in joy, too. "Napoleon will give us back Lithuania," they shout. "He gave the Poles back their Warsaw."

The fools, they rush to see Lithuania's Savior, that little dog of a man. What he'd do but lead all those beautiful soldiers into the Czar's Maw. The Czar, he knew what to do, that one. He pickled them in the Russian snow before chewing them up and spitting them out.

When the little dog and his scrap of an army come back, the neighbors, where are they? Stewing inside, cursing his name. Me? I stand by the road and cry. Poor wisps of men. The rags of uniforms barely stick to what's left. Can barely walk. I'd offer myself if there was anything to hold in my legs.

The husband, the *Master*? Him, I don't think of. After the sixth baby died, the *Master*, he drowned in the river. Maybe by his own hand. I don't remember. At night, I lie on my straw. I don't think of him. No. I dream of the soldiers. To make a man hard with just a wink. What it was like to be wet. When all the good things were not yet, not ever, of this world.

I look at the girl's nipples. Still pale and small. Like a babe's. Poor thing.

"Me, I had many lovers."

"Really?"

"I picked the best one. When our babies died, it kilt him."

She wanted more, the girl. There wasn't any.

...

The *Master*, he plans the Coming Out for the spring. The seamstress comes. The man to teach the dance. The man to teach the speech. The woman to teach the manners. But not from Paris or Moscow. From Cracow. These gentlemen, this lady, they look at the girl and ask her age. I say nothing and pass them the rubles. They teach the girl. Me? I bathe her.

After the moon rises and falls, over and again, I see the *Master*.

"She's not ready."

He looks up from his papers. A little afraid, but of me. Like always.

"Her teachers say she excels. Even with her locution."

"No. She doesn't bleed."

Takes him a while, this man. Then it hits.

"But she's fifteen!"

Think he'd notice something. The girl, she has no curves. Not like her mother. Some men, maybe they don't look at their girls as anything but. Maybe he's a good one, this *Master*, for a Catholic.

"Next year."

The Master, he goes back to his papers.

"Next year then."

...

The teachers keep coming. I bathe the girl. Not just when the moon shines either. I soap between her legs. I soap her chest. Nothing.

I tell her about the monthly blood. That soon, so soon, the blood will come for her.

"From the third arm?"

"Eh?"

"The third arm brings the blood."

I look at *her* now. Deep in her eyes. Sometimes you can see the soul wrestling a devil in the twinkle. This girl? Nothing. She's long, lank, but there's only child in her eyes.

"Never you mind," I say.

"Will Father buy me a new doll when he goes to Warsaw?"

...

Me? I search the manor over for the snakes. The estate for the dragon scat. Nothing. The peasant at the coop I ask about roosters in the house. She scoffs. I raise welts on her back with the switch.

"No, no! Never a rooster. *Never!*"

I'm still hot from the switching. I grab a rooster. Twist its neck and hold it under my foot till it stops moving. I'll let it stew, stew for hours.

Some time then, days, maybe weeks later at table, the mother, she cries out.

"My child. My sweet little mushroom. Come to me, Jagienka!"

The girl, she goes, like she does when the mother calls for her, it happens so rarely. She sits in her lap. Me, I step from the shadows and watch. The *Master*? He looks now at the girl, up and down. She's too big to sit on a mother's lap. With no curves. This anyone can see. The mother, she just fawns on the girl, presses her hair. Kisses her eyes. Like she's a child. Even though the girl has to bend into her.

Later, the *Master*, he calls for me. He paces. Back and forth. The papers on the desk flutter from the wind.

"She is ready now?"

He wants that to be the truth. I say nothing.

"But, but she is sixteen! A woman. How can this be?"

I shrug. "She isn't right."

Pacing. Back and forth.

"Impossible. Just impossible. She's growing. She's taller than her mother."

Impossible. This, from a man who prays to a god born of a virgin. A god split in three. Who died but isn't dead.

I wait. For hours? Who knows. The *Master*, he finally stops pacing. Sits on the edge of the desk. Puts his head in his hands.

"What happened?" I ask.

"What?"

"When the Cossacks came."

He moves his hands. Looks at me.

"What does that have to do with the child?"

I say nothing. Just look and wait. Who knows how long.

Then the *Master*, he talks. How he comes home the next day. How he finds the broken furniture, the crockery. How his wife is in blood, breathing, yes, but not alive. How he searches and searches for the girl. Finally finds her asleep, in the chest.

"In the room with the mother?"

Yes, he says. How he picks her up. How he carries her to bed. How she wakes up later, wanting her Name Day cake. Like nothing happened.

"She was fine."

I say nothing.

"The soldiers didn't touch her. They never saw her."

I say nothing.

"They didn't touch her. How could this be? How could this be the reason for, for what's... not happening?"

"As good as any."

...

I bathe her. The *Master*, he paces outside the kitchen. Always. Sometimes, I see his eye in the keyhole. Or hear his weeping. Like a woman. These men, these Cossacks, take his woman, his wife. Kill the woman in his child. He does nothing.

I scrub the girl till she cries out.

"Laume!"

I go soft. The *Master*, he can do nothing. He's good. For a Catholic. The Cossacks, they take what they want.

The girl? No man will want her. The convent? That god will reject her.

This girl. This woman. This still-born.

She has nothing. No future.

I love her as my own.

...

The teacher for dance? For the manners? The speech? All gone. No Mass either. The priest, he comes some nights, says the prayers in the darkened chapel while the family, the three, listen in shadows. After, I give the priest his rubles, tell him to keep his hole shut.

No one else comes. Not even friends of the *Master* are invited. Even at the holidays. I stop sprinkling the Tartar's kasha with the ground carrot seeds. He needs something, this *Master*. He's turning, like the mother. Going quiet. Like a specter. I feed him the milt, the pickled egg.

The girl? Soon, she stops asking after the "Coming Out." Maybe she knows she isn't right. But not how. Not why. She goes to the *Master's* library. Her face buried in those books. For hours even. Me? I have to drag her out for the supper.

…

I bathe her. The girl, she's the same. *The Master*? He no longer bothers to look through the keyhole.

"Were there 'Troubles' in Lithuania?"

"Always."

"I read about them."

"Stupid girl! Then why ask?"

My back. My knees. My whole body is beginning to ache. I bend. I scrub.

"Your father… did he, did he fight?"

My father? These Poles, they love to fight. They go across the ocean to die. For a country not even theirs. They take the drink and then they fight. My father? The first *Master*, he's no different. Always sending us away, so he can fight. When the little French dog comes back, here's the Czar, right behind him. My neighbors? They know the score, the way they cheered the snail eaters. My father? Him too. The neighbors? They run for the woods, with us in tow. To scramble in the bushes for berries and acorns. My father, the *Master*, he stays. Stands up to the Czar.

Just bones now. Planted in Lithuania? Siberia? Who knows.

Did he fight? I look in her eyes, the girl's. Something wrestles there I think.

"No. He was a good father. Like yours."

...

At table, the three, they eat. That's it. Quiet as a tomb. Except for the flatware touching the plates. Like spades hitting the rocks in the dirt.

The girl, she shifts in her seat. Something drops to the floor. The *Master*, he looks once, then again.

He bends, snatches it before she can. A pamphlet? Like the kind my husband, the *Master*, showed me sometimes to get me wet?

"Where did you get this?"

The girl, she stands. To her full height.

"Please, Father. I just wanted to read it."

"If they find this... If this is found... here. Or any of the others. God have mercy!"

"No one will find it. I'll burn it when I finish. Please, Father. You can watch me burn it."

"Mushroom!" Now the mother. "Would you like your cake now?"

The *Master*, he drops the pamphlet on the table. Buries his head in his hands.

"Of course. The cake. We must have the cake."

...

The pamphlet? I find others hidden in her bed clothes. Maybe from the *Master's* library she gets them. No pictures, though. Not like the ones to get the man hard, the woman wet. Only words. No use to me. "God have mercy," the *Master*, he said. He'd be angry. But who else can read? The mother? She's a ghost. The priest.

I give him a pamphlet, with the rubles. More than usual. I tell him to keep his hole shut about it after.

"What's it for?"

He sighs, this priest, this man with the three-pronged god.

"Where did you get it?"

"Never you mind."

This priest sighs once more.

"It's a call to arms. Again. You should dispose of it immediately."

"The others, too?"

Sigh.

"Of course. After what happened here last time, the rebels presume your master would be, well, at least sympathetic to their cause. The Russians will think the same."

I say nothing. The *Master*, he plans to fight with these rebels? Against the Czar? This Poland, this country that once was, is mad. Mad as Lithuania.

"Look for the red." The priest again. "If a door is painted red, your master is marking himself a rebel. Maybe he'll fight, or maybe he'll supply them. In any case, if you see the red, take the girl. Anywhere. I'll see about a convent, in the mountains..."

Madness. All of it. I take the pamphlets from the bedclothes, burn them to nothing. I scour the estate for others. Threaten to beat the Tarter, the milkmaid, the swineherd... No more pamphlets. Ever.

...

The peasants? They talk of the new "Troubles." In whispers. But I know. All know now. At night, after the family, the three, are sleeping, I check each door for the red. A brush and paint ready to cover it.

...

I bathe the girl.

"Soon, the Eye-talian will come and teach you to sing."

She smiles, the girl.

"And the Caucasian to teach you the dishes. And, and the Venetian for something ..."

"Yes, they will come soon. Won't they, Laume."

"Your husband? A French Prince."

She pats my hand. Smiles.

...

In the sleep, in my head, I bend. My back? My knees? No pain. Like I'm a girl again, swinging in the oak. I bend all the way, til my lips touch the earth.

"My Mother, the Master, you have given me life. You feed me. You carry me, and after death I will rest in you." And I do, down in the warm, blessed ground, bringing seven little babies to my breast.

The cock crows. I rise from the hay. My back. My knees. All cry at me. I creep down the stairs, through the kitchen. Out the door to draw the water. I pump and pump. The sun a sliver in the distance. Yawning, I turn and there. The red. On the back door.

I run, knees still crying at me. All the way to his room, the *Master's*. His snoring, like a bear's, so loud through the door. Still, I open up, go to the bed. I have to see. Do I smile? Maybe. But as I fall to my sore knees, in blessed relief, something clicks.

Me? I don't have to go to her room. I know. Only thing there, maybe, piles of her locks. The truth pulled from my inside.

The girl.

The seventh.

She's gone.

III.

The full moon in the cloudless sky is a mixed blessing. For once we are not blind men, feeling our way from bush to tree, stumbling over fallen branches or crashing through frozen rivulets. With the beams reflecting from the snow, nothing is hidden from our eyes: tracks of the bison; smoke from a small, distant fire snaking to the silent stars; a bloodied, half-eaten hare left by the crows until daybreak.

We ourselves are just as visible in the moon's glare. "Beaver" and "Moose" bring up the rear, dragging branches of pine to cover our steps through the snow.

"Cow" refuses to take his turn with the pine branches. According to him, the soldiers are not following, have no reason to. If any of us are left come spring, he maintains, they will pick us off when we try to leave the forest.

"Not to worry, boys," he told us so long ago, when the snows started to fall. "The wolves might get us first. If the soldiers? It'll be Siberia. The belly of the wolf, or the belly of the bear? Take your pick."

Even if the soldiers follow, having sight again seems a gift. What is truly worse is the cold. No wind bites at us, but we might consider that blessed relief. At least with the wind we might feel our faces and fingers. The unfettered moon seems to generate the cold like sun the heat.

Three hours past sundown, we make camp. If you can call it that. We still do not chance a fire; even "Cow" does not raise objections to this. We have not eaten in two days, and that was but a meager handful each of rotted potato peelings from a farmer's compost pile. We keep away the sting of hunger with snow. We try not to talk of the food, simply march until we are too tired to do it any longer. Then, the thirteen of us huddle around the base of a tree. For the semblance of preparedness, or simply out of habit, we examine our flasks each night for moisture and repack the powder in our guns.

We could split apart into smaller groups and find adjacent trees; certainly this would be more comfortable, and just as warm as the pile of groaning flesh and flailing limbs we become. Despite our bickering, however, we cling together as we cling to life, as if tomorrow has already passed, and the creatures we share our last few hours with are all we have left of ourselves.

...

This night, like all others, I keep the boy close to me, petting the fair, matted hair under his cap, waiting for the tears that never come. The fire that grows in me is the only thing bringing me warmth. How I want to impart this blaze on the boy, if only to warm his bones, to hold him here, to keep him from sliding into the dark.

...

When the moon is at its peak, the first wolf call pierces the silence. This, followed by another, from the opposite direction. Our eyes shutter open. Now more wolves howl in the night, until it seems we are surrounded. We untangle ourselves, brandishing the few weapons we managed not to drop during the battle: three hunting rifles, two pistols, two sabers, and an odd assortment of hunting and kitchen knives. We do this without comment and conflict; we've become so accustomed to it. Every night the wolves call, every night we wake, forming a circle around our chosen tree, weapons at the ready.

The wolves, however, keep their distance. Some of us suspect that they are not hunting us, but the bison we ourselves are trying to track.

"The night we don't watch is the night they'll come," Moose says.

"Let them come tonight," Cow says. "Soon enough we'll be skin and bones. Might as well give them a proper meal."

"Mouse" catches his breath then releases it. Even under the darkness of the pine we can see how his breath coats the dueling pistol he bears, how it becomes a fine layer of frost. We still wait to see some semblance of a beard on him, some indication that he is of age. We gave him the name "Mouse" because he squeaks like one during his sleep.

He is yet to say a word. Some of us speculate that the witch living at the L______ Estate cast a spell on him. He might even be the witch's bastard. Who knows? We all had reservations about him joining us—he seemed so young, so fragile—but he brought with him a rifle, plenty of powder and shot. Besides, this is a revolution for all people. Who will deny death to even the weakest man?

It was clear at the beginning, however, that he had no sense of how to use the rifle, had probably never fired it in his life, that he could not even load it properly. Beaver traded him one of his dueling pistols for it, and with much patience schooled him in the art of loading, shooting, and reloading.

Some of the men have said that Mouse will be the first offered to the wolves, if that is what it comes down to. What's the chance of him surviving the winter? If he can appease the hunger of the wolves for even a day or two, just long enough for the rest to slip away, so be it.

"Goat" senses this, or maybe he has heard things. We watch him sit close to the boy under the pine, notice that, during the day, he is only a step behind him, constantly watching his back. Goat is a big man. During the battle, he killed two of the enemy, crushing their windpipes with his thick fingers. None of us want to think of those fingers around our own necks.

"Do you have a preference, Mouse?" Cow asks, prodding the boy with his frayed boot. "The Bear or the Wolf?"

Always the same question, but the boy never answers. We laughed at first, but now we squirm against each other, doing our best to find a comfortable spot on the fallen branches and crackling leaves.

"Leave him be," Goat says. As always.

Like other nights, the cries of the wolves eventually fade, as do we, into the arms of sleep and whatever comfort it brings.

...

Their eyes eventually close and their breaths lengthen. All but Cow, who has the watch. Despite his cynicism, he's in it until the end. Like me, he was raised on the tales of Kosciuszko, how, with only peasants armed with scythes and pitchforks, he defeated the Czar's army at Raclawice.

There will be no such glory for me, or for Cow, or for the boy. My only hope is that the revolt still blazes elsewhere.

"Would you pass the tobacco?" Cow whispers across the ring of sleeping bodies.

"Fresh out," I say. "I'll stop at the tobacconist's in the morning."

Cow chuckles. The boy's eyes pop open and look up at me. My heart clenches. He burrows deeper into my side. His hands are wrapped in rags, but his fingertips are bare. My first impulse is to put them into my mouth, to coax the blood back to the surface. Heat rises in my cheeks, staining them red. I grab both his hands, pressing them palm to palm in a state of prayer and slide them into my arm pit. His eyes close once again, and soon the throbbing in his fingers lessens.

I want to follow him into sleep, but fear glues open my eyes. Not fear of the wolves, or of the Russians, but that unnamed thing in my very depth, the gnawing monster that paralyzed even Saint Augustine. In the lighted hours, my comrades keep awake my reason, even if it be but a reason nourished by fear of ridicule and disdain.

But in the dark hours? Reason's eyes close with the eyes of the body...

...

"We're still of this earth," Cow says.

We stand, stamping our feet, blowing into our stiff hands. The sun has risen, shimmering through the thin clouds that spread across the sky like locks of hair on a noblewoman's shoulders.

What does not remind us of sausages and stews thick with gravy, dense bread and crumbly white cheese, reminds us of fair-skinned ladies waltzing across finely polished floors, gloved fingertips fluttering on our shoulders, or better yet, plump peasant women who, for the right coin, will satiate our most wanton hungers.

It is our need for all flesh that drives us deeper into the Bialowieza Forest. This will get us past the frost bite and the wolves, for when we no longer hunger, what? We all fear that point of no return, when our stomachs no longer growl, and our loins no longer burn. We might still be standing upright, but whatever part of us was once men will fall to the wayside like old apples dropping from the tree.

"I had a vision last night," Sheep says. "The Madonna came to me."

"The Madonna, eh?" Cow says. "The Madonna in winter? I heard she doesn't like the snow. Consider where she's from. But do tell."

Sheep stammers and rubs his pointed chin. "The Madonna... she showed me the bison..."

"Again, consider where she's from. There were no bison in Bethlehem. Sheep, yes. Would the Madonna know what one looked like? But who am I to judge."

"Please," Goat says. "Let him finish."

We all want to hear him finish. Perhaps even Cow. What else do we have but visions in the dark?

"She told me... there's one injured... she told me to go that way." Sheep points to a spot that looks like any other. There is no discernable path, no clearing just beyond the veil of trees; just branches, and snow, and a near future no different than the near past.

"That's it then," Cow says. "Let's hope the Madonna has mead for us on the other end."

And so we march once again, but with the branches and the hidden roots we might as well be blind and drunk. A straight line is impossible. Still we follow Sheep, even when the clouds cover the sun, and the snow once again begins to fall through the naked oaks and the naked elms. As the flakes bite into what remains of our clothing, each one of us thinks back to the last night of warmth, so many weeks, or so many months, ago.

We engaged the enemy a week before that night, and when we few thirteen were severed from the main force, we ran together without awareness of who was amongst us. There was just our burning calves, and the fear of the horses in pursuit, and finally, the sanctuary of the cover of night. Only then did we take stock of our comrades, and the situation we were in. We vowed then not to use our real names, even amongst ourselves, in case any of us was captured.

Over those seven days, farmers, some totally unaware of the revolution, fed us and housed us, treating us with a kindness that made us forget, if only for a moment, the warmth of our own homes and families. An elderly couple who had lost all their children before even one reached adulthood boarded us in the horse barn of their master's estate. The horses themselves had been commandeered by the Russians some weeks before, but the couple had cleaned the stalls and laid down fresh hay in hope that their charges would one day return. They brought us bread, sausage, and watered beer. And though we complained amongst ourselves then that the bread was a day old, and the beer was too weak, we now thought about the meal and the beds with a longing so acute that it dulled the pain, if only for a moment, of our throbbing stomachs and our frozen limbs.

...

I knew, the night before we entered the forest. What I knew I couldn't say, for I was a man, and he would one day be a man, and there was nothing in my past to prepare me. My belly was full, and the hay beneath me was firm and fresh, and sometime during the night he sidled up next to me. Or maybe he had always been there. I don't know. At one point, the door to the horse barn creaked open. I don't think anyone besides myself and the boy actually noticed. A man and a woman, whispering and giggling, squeezed through the door and shut it behind them.

Who were they? Swineherd and milkmaid? Master and cook? Whoever they were, they quickly relieved themselves of their nightclothes. Moonlight beamed through the unpaned window above them, illuminating their naked bodies in an ethereal glow. At first they were rough with each other, pinching and teasing, kissing then backing away, but all the time giggling. When the woman reached for the man, making him grow big in her hand, the boy next to me loudly exhaled and began to shake. The woman continued to stroke her lover. The boy mumbled something under his breath. I pulled him closer and cupped his mouth and jaw in my hand. Still he shook. I was fully prepared to pinch closed his nose and end his life. Who knew how sympathetic these two would be to us?

The woman stopped and looked in our direction.

"Don't stop," her lover said. "Please."

She crooned, her loose hand drawing his mouth to hers. They kissed deeply. Suddenly, the games they were playing were over. They tumbled into each other, onto the bare dirt in front of the door, enveloping, moving, like two people not in lust, but very much in love.

The boy then stopped shaking. I somehow knew that he would be okay, and removed my hand from his mouth, but I kept my arm on his back as we both watched the man and woman ensconced in a rapture so complete they were totally oblivious to not only us, but to the war raging just beyond the next hill, the next stand of trees.

Initially, I never felt so alone, watching these two lovers. I was a man on the run, everyone I cared for now in another world. My future, what could it be? My life seemed nothing more than what I had already lived.

There was just the now. The boy. His body against my own. Perhaps this would be the last warmth I would ever know.

...

Two days after Sheep's vision, "Raven" and "Otter" drop, nearly simultaneously. We have no shovels to dig at the frozen earth, no stand of stones to pile on top of them. The most we can do is kick away a shallow patch of snow and lay them side to side, but not before we strip them of every bit of clothing to add to what we have of our own. We look down at their bruised, emaciated bodies, the distended stomachs, the broken fingernails, arms and legs like the brittle branches of dead trees.

We turn away, not out of distaste, but because we all know we are the same under the rags we wear. Whatever has taken their lives will soon take ours. We mumble prayers we know no god will hear, scooping snow over the bodies.

"The wolves will take them," Cow says, without callousness or sarcasm. It is a simple statement of fact. We have to put distance between ourselves and the bodies by nightfall.

"Sheep?" Moose says. "Where to?"

Sheep turns and puts one foot forward. We follow.

...

The night in the horse barn, after the couple had left and even the boy had fallen to slumber, I pleasured myself. In my mind's eye I saw the naked woman only, but I was very much aware of the boy breathing slowly next to me, his arm exerting an exquisite pressure on my side. The memory of the experience kept my physical needs at bay for some days, but once or twice, in the night, I awoke to a stickiness in my drawers.

That doesn't happen now. Lust has gone the way of my hunger: a sharp memory and nothing more. I think back to that other life, that other place, that other time, and the students who were charged to me. Certainly I was fond of them, even those I did not like. I saw them as a student body, not as individuals. As time passed, their names changed, as did their faces, but on the first day of each term, I walked into the lecture hall, looked upon them, and my fondness spread from my open arms and encompassed them all.

I want to think what I felt for the boy is what I felt for all the boys I have ever taught. But no. Even after we bury the two, I look at him and something inside of me, something immovable, gives way. Like the stone blocking the tomb of the Christ. Even now, as our time grows short, I want to argue with Diderot and Voltaire.

See, there is a caring God.

Of course, they say, you're on death's threshold. All believe in such a god then.

No, it's not for me. What does it matter what happens to me. It's for him. Only God could make me love now.

...

We chew on twigs and hollow acorns to appease our hunger. Whatever sustenance we gain drips from our loose bowels. Still, we shuffle through the drifting snow, bodies bent into the wind. No matter the direction we take, the wind blows against us. We do not know who the weakest amongst us is since we unconsciously fall into step with the slowest.

The wolves still call, and the bison still evade us, and soon, we are down to eight.

...

As I kick the snow over the dead I look at the boy, in wonder that he is still upright.

But how couldn't he be? He's my heart. If his were to stop beating, I would soon follow. How long would it take? If only a few seconds, it would still seem an eternity. For once I curse my physical strength, my stamina. Oh God, let me be the first to go.

...

We lose track of the days since Sheep's vision. No one knows the week, let alone the month, and if pressed, we might not know the year. Still, we follow, even after another fails to wake up one morning. On the same day, some hours after we stripped the body, Sheep stops, falls to his knees and bows his head.

We think we have lost another. But no, not yet.

"Moose," Cow whispers. "Your rifle."

The rest of us peer through the trees, finally dropping as if in prayer, and there, in a small clearing, stands a lone bison, its back end towards us.

"Aim for a back leg," Goat says. "Right above the knee. It's the only way to stop it."

Moose lowers his aim. When the rifle begins to waver, Cow scoots in front to offer his shoulder for leverage.

We wait, and we wait. But perhaps only a few seconds elapses before Moose squeezes off the shot. And then the explosion of the rifle, loud enough to crack ice. We haven't heard a sound much louder than a whisper for many months, and now this, shaking the very air itself.

The bullet shatters the bison's thigh bone. Its head juts towards the sun and lets loose a deep, baritone bellow. The body moves, seemingly of its own volition, but the other back leg collapses before it can complete one step.

In a blur, Goat zigzags through the trees, pulling a knife from somewhere deep in the rags he wears.

"Follow!"

And we do, our aches, our pains, our grief spilling to the ground in the promise of our quarry.

Goat clears the last of the trees and leaps upon the back of the bison. His momentum drives the animal to the ground. He grabs one horn, twisting its head to expose the neck to the brandished knife.

We catch up, dropping to our knees. The breaths of bison and Goat combine into puffs in the still air.

"I am going to cut the throat," Goat says, "and each one of us will drink. Only then will we be able to keep down the meat."

As he draws the knife across the flesh, he reaches up with one long arm and pulls down Mouse's face, burying it in the bison's muzzle, even while the creature's eye still blinks in terror and pain. The beast blows breath through its quivering nostrils as the boy sucks the life from its jugular. We hear every drop of its blood pass over his tongue, down his throat, into his waiting belly. Our own stomachs grumble. We lick our lips, each one of us wanting to kick away the boy.

...

Drink, for this is my blood...

...

When the blood fountains over the head of the still drinking boy, Moose joins him, and once both can hold no more, the rest of us take our fill, like puppies at the teat. Sticky and satiated, we fall to the snow. No longer does it seem too cold on our backs. The life of the bison coats the back of our throats, the walls of our stomachs. If before we dreamt of white creamy potatoes, pale green cabbage, the dense orange of carrots, now the images fluttering in our minds are of duck blood soup, boiled beets, plump strawberries right off the plant. We swim in a river of red. Our minds, our faces, our clothes, the ground, even the trees are stained red. Now, there is no more beautiful color in the world.

Stomachs quieted, bowels beginning to tighten, we lift ourselves from the red snow and look towards our savior. The heat of its death melts the snow so now the bison lay on bare ground, the mud beneath it tinged red. The eye, a polished black opal, stares at us in defeat. One drop of blood travels slowly down the opening in the neck before dropping to the ground. We lick our lips, mopping up the blood settled in the cracks.

...

Eat, for this is my body.

...

There is only a brief discussion about the fire. Cooking the meat is a secondary consideration. We would gladly eat it raw. The sun is beginning to fall. The first wolf call sounds closer than it has in many nights. The fire, we hope, will keep them at bay. And if the Russians see the glow? What of it. At least we will have some strength in our bones when they come.

We spend two days in that small clearing, tearing into roasted flesh. Even when our bodies at first reject it, we continue to feast. Meanwhile, we dry the hide and slice it into squares that we tie around what remains of our boots. Where the bison once lay, we dig a pit and build a fire with leaves and acorns, and smoke strips of the meat. Moose stretches and cleans the guts for casings for the minced innards.

"The king would be very disappointed in us," Cow says.

We blink, him sitting there, patting his belly. And then we get the joke. Bialowezia was once the royal hunting ground for kings of old. We laugh and raise imaginary mugs of honey mead, as if we are hunters, out one Saturday morning for some sport with our closest comrades.

...

Blood has come back to his cheeks, but they remain smooth as plums. Neither is there a sign of whisker on his lip. I feel like a beast next to him, as wild and untamed as the thing we eat. For a moment, as we sit around the fire, I no longer see the darkened trees, no longer scan the distance for the eyes of the wolves. The forest coalesces into the paneled walls of my room at university. I sit in my favorite chair, a crystal glass of brandy on the table, reading Pushkin aloud. The boy is at my feet, looking up at me in wonder.

...

We force ourselves to leave. The little clearing has been the closest thing to home since our night in the horse barn. Why not stay, build a cabin, wait for the spring to plant?

Each one of us ponders this, ridiculous as it sounds. Now that we have caught the bison, we have no other goal. The call to arms is but a distant memory. Nature has taken the six we left scattered behind us, so where is the need for vengeance? Are we to hunt down the wolves that tore through their earthly remains?

Once we had homes and loved ones, but who knows if we can ever reenter those past lives. Outside these woods, the world may be nothing but a smoldering ruin. All we have left then is the hike, the hiding of our traces, the smothering of our footprints. But can Man survive for evasion alone?

A week after we leave the bones of the bison for the wolves, the weather begins to change. The bare sun sets our clothes steaming. Water drips from the trees. The snow is thick and sticky under our feet. It becomes impossible to hide our tracks.

Within the span of a day we realize that winter, our greatest enemy, has also been our greatest ally. What will stop the soldiers from pursuing us now? And how can we walk unnoticed in any village, unshaven, encased in ragged clothes and bits of untreated hide? The very idea of removing the clothing frightens us, since we do not know if the flesh still clinging to our bones will come with it.

The temperature continues to climb. We look to the sun and allow the beams to curve around our faces. At some point, when the trees grow narrow and closer together, we hear a trickling of water. With no other destination at hand, we kick through the snow towards the sound, anything to hide the shape of a foot. The trees part, revealing sheets of transparent ice over a moving stream. We follow its banks for well over an hour until it dips into a small ravine. Small pools are still covered in thin ice, but now water rushes freely, downward over large stones and fallen branches. The banks rise higher and higher on either side of the stream.

"This might take us to the River Bug," Cow says.

We walk carefully on the rocks, downstream, and when night falls, we rest against the left bank. A slight overhang has kept it free from snow and ice. Call it instinct, but we immediately take inventory of our weapons, then clean the barrels of the guns and sharpen the knives on exposed rocks. Not until the weapons are gleaming at our side, powder and charge in place, do we chew on the strips of bison and dip our chapped hands into the water running before us.

Below us the stream rounds a bend before flattening and losing its momentum, once again lazy and covered in ice. The right bank gives way to a broad, snow-covered shore in front of the woods. The trees are spaced out, providing access to horses.

This does not occur to us until the next morning.

...

During my watch I burn. Was it the food? The spring weather? Or the boy's breath on my thigh? I strain against my trousers, the warmth of him passing over and over as he sleeps like the dead, his mouth slightly ajar, enough that I can make out his bottom teeth even here in the dark. The heat once opening my heart spreads down to my lap, towards his mouth and his twitching hands. If I were to only...

To what? How am I to know. To press his naked body to mine. Perhaps that would be enough.

The boy on one side of me, my bare knife on the other. I reach down and grab it, squeezing until the blade cuts into my palm. The sweet pain keeps me awake until dawn.

...

At the first sign of light we eat, and then we drink from the stream. Who is the first to hear the neighing of horses? Perhaps all of us at once, for suddenly we scramble for our weapons and the scraps of meat, not at first sure of where the sound comes from, or what direction we are to take. After months of marching and near starvation, this is the first sign of our pursuers, if they are even that. Maybe it's nothing but a gentleman out for a morning ride.

But no. Now we hear the hooves in the dirt, through the snow. There are many of them, too many to count. Suddenly five mounted soldiers appear on the riverbank, down below us, not more than fifty yards away. We freeze. Our way downstream blocked, the banks on either side of the stream too steep to quickly climb. The only option is back up, over the rushing water and slippery rocks.

After all this time, the frost-bitten fingers and toes, the collapsed bowels, the loss of hair, of teeth, of fingernails, the deaths of our comrades, all of it comes to this. Each one of us to be picked off by marksmen or made captive and sent to the endless cold of Siberia.

Still, we are frozen. How many minutes pass before the officer at the head of the line of soldiers looks up and sees us? And what does he first imagine, us with our tattered clothes, our unshaven faces? Some kind of new beast?

He gives out a shout and draws his saber, as do the other four. Then more soldiers appear on the banks, pulling their rifles from their shoulder holsters.

We look back upstream, and then down. One of us starts to weep. Then Goat, the strongest among us, does the most unusual thing. Years later, we will still question what we see. He turns, bent forward, grasps Mouse's head in his large, beefy hands, and plants a kiss on his lips.

Time stops. We look in wonder, as do the soldiers below us. And then Goat is gone, in a blur, rushing down the stream, skipping across the round slippery stones, drawing his knife, a most unnatural cry flying from this throat.

The officer raises his saber even higher, spurs his horse to charge Goat. The sun glints off the golden epaulets, and the saber raised, gleaming, looks to us like the wing of an angel.

Mouse aims his dueling pistol. Don't waste the shot, we want to shout. The distance is too great. But before we can, before Cow pulls him away, he squeezes the trigger, the pop of the gun turning into an explosion between the high banks. A split second later, blood blossoms, like a handful of red carnations, out the back of the officer's head. The reins still firmly tied in his right hand, his body falling backward, the momentum of the bullet stronger than that of his ride. The horse rears up, eyes bulging, front hooves flaying for purchase inches from Goat's face. But now, off balance, the weight of the colonel is too much. Both rider and mount tumble into the stream, and even from up high, we hear the bones crack.

Mouse turns to us, arm and pistol still pointed toward the enemy. Something opens. No whiskers. The descending cheek bones, the blond locks spilling out of her cap. The hint of a bosom.

After all these months, we see who she is.

"Run!" Goat shouts. We look back. He holds the colonel's saber. Another soldier lay before him. He reaches down, rips the pistol from the soldier's hand and fires into the chest of another. Dozens of others shout, swinging their sabers, bringing their rifles to bear.

She takes a step down, down towards Goat and the fate he is about to meet. Somehow he knows. He turns back, his face twisted in fury.

"Run!"

Cow puts his arm around her gut.

"Come," he says gently. "Come, for his sake. He's finished."

...

Fly, my love. Fly like the wind.

...

Mouse relents and turns. We scramble back up the stream as wildly aimed shots ping against the rocks. Soon we are around the bend, out of view of the soldiers, though we still hear their shouts and the clanging of metal. We all know Goat will not last long, but he gives us the time. The stream levels, the banks diminish and the trees grow thick.

It would be easier to join our comrade in the clearing, to end it all right now in a bloody flourish. For what lay ahead on this other path? Pain and starvation. The wrenching loneliness of life on the run. This futile gesture of revolt against a force greater than that of the Almighty. But we reenter the woods and do not look back, knowing we will fight on, if for no other cause than the nobility of man.

THIRST

The day began like all spring days leading up to the fertility festivals. The soldiers of the guard sat high in their fortress, watching over the young girls who sought wildflowers in the fields just outside the walls while in the town center their mothers, babies tied to their backs, roamed the streets seeking out the choicest cuts of venison. These women kept a careful eye on their husbands who swaggered around their carts of pelts and wild hare, while at their side dirtied sons grabbed the skirts of the slower passersby and shouted prices up to wary smirks. All the meandering paths and roads led the townspeople to the square, which bustled with flower peddlers and tool hawkers, and rang with the blacksmith's hammer and the woodcutter's saw. The men soon took their business into the taverns, and the women gathered in small circles to discuss potential husbands for their oldest daughters.

Suddenly, the sky grew dark. The townspeople looked up to where the sun should have been. It had been said that once the moon, grown jealous of the sun's reign over man, leapt from night to day and brought darkness when there should have been light. The townspeople thought that this time had come again, for a black ball had replaced the sun, and not one of them could remember seeing the moon the night before. The taverns and shops emptied and then all stood transfixed, eyes pinned to the sky as the air around the black orb coalesced and swirled. Still, they remained in the square, even as the orb sprouted wings, shot flame and dove towards them. Only once the apparition was nearly upon them did the spell break. Then they realized that this vision descending upon them was a dragon, a creature they before had only encountered in the lyrics of wandering minstrels. The crowd dropped their wares and scattered, running in terror for the warren of alleyways spreading away from the square.

A beggar who had many winters earlier lost his toes to the greening, straggled behind the rest of the crowd. The dragon snatched him with yellow claws and soared back into the sky. The beggar's screams soon receded into the distance, but the monster wheeled back, and then fell again, towards the wooden fortress. It hovered for a moment above the river before settling gently on the bank. The gypsies who lived in the cave directly in front of the dragon poured from their home. The creature paid them no heed. It set on the beggar, stripping him first of the rags on his back, and then of the flesh from his bones. The dragon ate quickly but methodically, showing little interest in the dying groans of his victim, or the fading cries of the gypsies. Once all the flesh had been consumed, the creature cracked apart the largest bones and sucked out the marrow. It then yawned and crawled into the cave. Soon the remnants of the gypsy household—pots, clothes, patchwork quilts and firewood flew from the mouth of the cave. The creature settled in and fell asleep, the rumble of its snores shaking the wooden foundations of the fortress above.

The son of the captain of the guard had the wherewithal to seek out his father, who, at the moment of attack, lay comfortably in the arms of his mistress. The boy pushed open the door of the one room cottage and shouted, "Dragon!" The captain pulled himself from bed, rubbing the sleep from his eyes.

"Dragon!" the boy cried again. "It will kill us all!"

"Dragon," the captain snorted. "Go home to your mother, boy."

The captain was a strong and courageous man, and since his ascension to power, very few marauders tempted their fate by attacking the town, and those that did soon found their heads on pikes above the main gate. Dragon, indeed. To him, dragons lived in stories meant to scare children. Whatever this creature was, he would put an end to it soon enough. Within seconds he was again clad in leather armor. He made his way to the fortress, as townspeople sped past him, screaming and crying. He found his men in complete disarray. They had not witnessed the attack, and had yet to see the creature, but they all could feel it beneath their feet. The captain brought them to attention, and soon they hurriedly strapped on their armor and took up bows and swords. The captain ordered his men to pile dry wood in front of the cave. He himself stood above the mouth, sword in one hand, a lit torch in the other. Even while the ground beneath him shook, he showed no fear.

"Arrows!" he ordered.

His men formed a half circle fifteen feet from the pile of wood, just inches from the river, swollen from the melting snows in the hazy, distant mountains. They fit arrows to string and waited for the beast to emerge. Their eyes also showed no fear, for the soldiers had complete faith in their captain, and like him, they had no reason to think that any creature other than man could harm them.

The captain dropped the torch into the woodpile. Birch and elm immediately began to crackle and spit, and soon even the cold stone beneath the captain's feet became too hot for the soles of his leather boots. He climbed down the side of the hill and stood in wait beside his men. Above the sputtering flames, they heard a bellow, and then something like the yawn of a bear emerging from its winter sleep. The captain and his men relaxed; they had all killed bear one time or another.

In that brief moment, when the soldiers' muscles loosened and sighs escaped from their throats, the creature appeared in front of them. It had made no noise when it emerged from the cave. There it was, sitting in the middle of the inferno the captain thought would drive it out. Coals glowed red between its toes, and flames danced around its drawn wings. Smoke trickled out of its long snout, and the light from the fire reflected off its scaled belly and neck. Even though the men had never seen a dragon before, in fact, never believed such things existed, they all mouthed the word, "dragon."

"N-now," the captain croaked.

Twenty arrows flew. The ones that hit their mark, square in the dragon's breast, snapped like kindling in high summer. Flame then erupted from the dragon's mouth. Before the captain's men were reduced to piles of ash, they saw the coal black eyes of the dragon change to red. The force of the dragon's breath blasted the captain into the river. He landed on the surface, clutching the arm that had been scorched. As he fought to keep his head above water, he saw the dragon bound to the spot where his men once stood. The creature bent its long neck towards the river and sent forth a sound that shook loose the leaves from the trees across the river. It looked once at the captain, now in his death throes as he sailed away slowly on the current, yawned, and then crawled back into its cave.

...

After nightfall, the elders convened a meeting in the feast hall. The wisest of the leaders remained silent until the shouts and cries of the townspeople died down. He knew that the choices for dealing with this situation were few. The best and bravest of the men were gone. There seemed to be no way of driving the dragon from its den with force. One of the townspeople suggested that they all leave and head for the mountains. But most were reluctant to abandon their fields and shops, and all feared the bandits who lived and preyed on those without an armed escort. Another suggested that the town would have to learn to live with the dragon, in the same way that it lived with the threat of Mother Earth expanding the waters of the Vistula into flood, or the clouds into blizzard and hail. The great dragon would become part of their natural lives and eventually would be no more terrible of a threat than pestilence or war. One farmer witnessed the attack at the cave. He maintained that the dragon had no desire to enter the river to finish off the captain. Perhaps it was afraid of water.

After much discussion the dark-skinned man from the south stepped in front of the crowd and approached the elders. The feast hall grew quiet.

The dark man had arrived six months earlier. Even though the town did not appreciate the sudden appearance of strangers, its people paid little attention to him at first, not even the captain of the guard, for the stranger arrived alone and carried no weapon. He minded his peace through the winter, lived in a lean-to outside the city walls with the shepherds and their flocks. It was with them he perfected the local way of speech, and by early spring he wandered the paths inside the walls, speaking of a man and a god and a ghost, all who had lived many years ago in a land too strange for most to believe. The High Priestess labeled him a heretic. The shepherds that knew him, however, as well as the prostitutes who had befriended him, defended the stranger's right to preach.

"He has great magic," the shepherds and prostitutes maintained. "Have you not noticed the wooden amulet around his neck, or the strange language he uses for his incantations?"

The townspeople had seen the amulet and heard the strange man mumble when he looked into a mysterious leather box, which contained smooth pieces of what looked like leather. On the leather were pictures that were not pictures.

Now, in the feast hall, the prettiest of all the prostitutes spoke:

"Do not fear his magic," she said. "For he is not a wizard, but a teacher. His "box" is a book, a device made known to us by travelers from the great cities of the west. It is not a book of spells, but of stories in the language of his people. Through his book I have learned about a place without fear or pain."

"Enough, woman," the stranger said, and raised his arms.

"Great elders. This beast comes from the bowels of the earth. In this place live thousands of others much larger and more fearsome than the beast in your cave. They wait for the command to rise from the earth and to sweep across your land in a torrent of fire. But, fear not."

The daughter of the town's baker opened her mouth and began to speak, but her father squeezed her shoulder and shook his head.

"This fool talks in riddles," he muttered.

The wisest of our elders slowly stood. The crowd gasped in astonishment; no one could remember when he last was able to use his feet.

"Then tell us, the one some call 'Teacher,'" he said. "Why should we not bow in fear when you tell us thousands of dragons will soon sweep across our lands?"

"You should not even fear these thousands of dragons," the stranger said, "for there are things far worse than death. You and all the people here may die from the dragons' breath, but once you are planted in the ground you will fall under the dominion of their Master. Under the control of the Master, you will live another thousand lives in a misery you cannot possibly imagine."

"Sacrilege!" another yelled. The crowd began to murmur vague threats.

The wisest elder frowned. He raised his arm, signaling for quiet.

"You come from a land far from here," the elder said to the dark man, "but even your people must know what lies beyond this life. I am not far from the Threshold. Soon I will be feasting with my forefathers, as will all these good people, under the grace of our Mother."

The stranger looked to the sky and grabbed the amulet around his neck.

"Soon they will know the Truth," he said quietly.

"Teacher," one person said. "If you anger the Master, will you conjure an army to fight the dragons of which you speak?"

"Like the beast in your cave," the stranger said. "I am but a messenger for my Master, the Father of the Heavens. Allow me to confront your beast, and my Master will hold dominion over you, both in this life and the next."

The crowd began to murmur once again. They did not want this man's ruler or his army here to protect them from a legion of dragons no one had ever seen. The townspeople began shouting at the prostitute, who responded with crazed notions of a one true God and a place in the sky called "heaven."

"You see what he promises us, Father!" the baker said. "Will you let his master control us?"

"Quiet!" the elder ordered.

When the room once again became silent he continued.

"Teacher," he said. "We respect your concern for our wellbeing and thank you for coming to us before acting on your own. You have given us proper due. Wait now and we will give our decision."

With this pronouncement, the stranger bowed. The elder sat in his oak litter and his bearers carried him away, to the anteroom, followed by the rest of the elders. The crowd suspected correctly that the High Priestess herself waited there to offer her advice.

When the elders returned to the hall, many hours later, only the stranger and prostitute remained. The townspeople did not know the outcome of the meeting until the next morning, when word spread that the stranger would be allowed to confront the dragon.

Unlike all other days, the square remained empty as the sun rose in the sky. The blacksmith, his eyes searching far above him, hurried to the baker and told him that he had seen the High Priestess return an hour earlier to the Sacred Grove. He was surprised of the elders' decision now, for the Priestess had appeared amused when she passed by. She should have been angry, he told the baker, for did not the stranger say the dragon came from the earth itself?

"Perhaps," the baker said, "she does not take his magic seriously."

Both men concluded, however, that the stranger would be the dragon's next meal. Better him than they.

Before the blacksmith left the bakery, the stranger, the prostitute and the elders entered the square. The elders settled themselves in chairs under the dubious shelter of a wooden overhang. The stranger and prostitute walked right into the middle of the square. The townspeople who lived in the cottages nearby poked their heads carefully out of doors and windows and watched. The stranger knelt on a piece of bark and spoke in his strange language. He remained in this position until the sun had scattered the morning clouds and sat high in the sky.

"You are afraid," the blacksmith shouted from his door. "Where is your precious master now? Is he sleeping away the afternoon?"

Much to the blacksmith's annoyance, the stranger ignored him. Eventually, he pulled himself up and smoothed his robes.

"Now it is time," he said. With his amulet firmly grasped in his hand, he started walking in the direction of the dragon's lair. The prostitute gasped and went to follow, but her teacher shook his head and continued on his own. He soon turned the corner, out of sight.

Hours passed. The elders shifted in their chairs. As more time slipped by, those who worked indoors returned to their tasks: shoeing a horse, milling grain, dyeing leather. Some joked, said the stranger took this opportunity to run for his life. As the sun continued on its way, even the elders started to leave their places, all but the wisest of them; he remained complacently in his chair.

At the moment all had given up, a piercing scream shattered the silence. A moment later the sky grew dark. Was it possible that the stranger's master was sending a message? Had the dragon been defeated? The prostitute, who had been waiting nervously for the return of the stranger, ran past the elder, hands raised in the air.

As it had the day before, the dragon appeared suddenly and sped towards the square, like a hawk that has spotted a hare in the wild grass. This time, the dragon took the prostitute with one set of claws, and as it ascended once again, it dropped from the other what was left of the stranger; his now tattered robe, a jumble of broken bones and finally, like an afterthought, his leather book, which landed inches from the elder's feet. The elder picked it up and flipped through the pages. The symbols meant nothing to him.

"It is done," he said. He stood and dropped the book to the ground, then shuffled through the square and out the northern gate. He was never heard from again.

...

The town would then see the darkest days of its young history. Some people tried to run for the mountains, but the dragon swept before them, driving them back inside the city walls, corralling them like sheep for the slaughter. The creature burned the fields and destroyed the herds. Those living outside the walls had no choice but to move into the town, which made food and water scarcer than before. Every day, one person disappeared from somewhere inside the walls. All knew the person's fate, and all prayed they would not be the dragon's next meal.

With meat in short supply, the townspeople were forced to rely entirely on the fish a brave few caught in the river and the meager supply of flour stored within the walls. The baker took on most of the trade. When his customers had nothing to barter, the baker gave them bread anyway. These hungry souls shuffled uneasily into the bakery and took their bread from the baker's daughter.

The daughter herself had always been a curiosity. Regardless of the strength of the light, her arms sparkled, so much so that she was referred to as the "Girl with Crystal Arms." The baker was not her natural father. Six months after his wife had passed away giving birth to a stillborn child, he spotted the girl in the woods not far from the town walls. Despite the denseness of the underbrush, she was easy to see, as her arms glowed brighter than the most polished gold. She approached him slowly. Once she was just paces away, a hare sprang out from the underbrush. The girl continued towards the baker, who took her by the hand. She became the child he had lost.

The household the baker and the girl established was a happy one. Initially, the baker hesitated at the idea of his adoptive daughter working by his side in the blasting heat of the shop, but for reasons he could not explain, any dough the young girl touched became enhanced with a flavor completely unknown to him. In fact, the bread she formed with her nimble, sparkling hands tasted better than any he had baked before her arrival. Soon the rest of the town discovered this as well, and together, father and daughter's product became a staple at tables all over town. Every morning, long before even the birds began to sing, a meandering line of customers lined the muddy alleyway in front of the shop, waiting patiently for the shutters to open.

Over the passing years, the baker sometimes speculated about the girl's parents. Perhaps they had abandoned her because of her strange arms, or maybe they had been killed in an ambush, and she had miraculously escaped. When he tried to question the girl about her life before he found her, she maintained that she did not remember a mother and father. Instead the pictures in her mind were only of a hole in a hillock close to where the baker had found her. She could not say what she had eaten, or what she had drunk; only that the hillock was her home, and that the walls inside sparkled like her arms. This she told him, but she never revealed why she had left the hillock; that a wild hare spoke, instructing her to seek out the company of humans.

Within weeks after the dragon's arrival, the baker began to limit to each family one loaf per day. Even though there was enough flour to last until harvest in a typical year, this year was not typical. It seemed unlikely that there would be wheat to grind come autumn, and now that the meat supply had been cut off, more and more people depended entirely on bread.

Occasionally, the blacksmith would stop and talk to the baker after he had received his loaf. They spoke of the latest people to disappear, and what, if anything, could be done about the dragon. The soldiers were gone, the elders were in disarray, and even the High Priestess remained absent, whether because she herself had been taken, or had retreated deeper into the forest, no one knew. The blacksmith often talked of the stranger from the south and wondered aloud if there was any truth to his tales. Even though he had heckled the stranger, he now wondered if his Master, angered at the killing of his messenger, would come from the sky and seek revenge against the dragon, thereby saving the town.

Once, the girl dared to speak:

"The stranger was wrong," she said. "The dragon did not come from the ground. It came from the east. I saw it. I was picking flowers that day. I saw that it came from the east."

The blacksmith and the baker looked sad then, because the girl's words dashed their only remaining hope.

One of the customers who had frequented the shop before the arrival of the dragon was a widow just a few years younger than the baker. The Girl with Crystal Arms knew little about the workings between man and woman, so she never drew conclusions about why the widow so often lingered to talk to her father. Not too soon after the widow's first trip to the shop, however, the baker began to leave once his daughter fell asleep. The dragon's arrival did not stop his nocturnal visits to the widow's cottage on the other side of the square, for the need of his flesh was stronger than his fear of being taken. And so it happened that one night after the baking, the girl's father left. This time, when she woke in the morning to open the shop, her father was simply gone. She called for him, tried to search the town, but the blacksmith restrained her. While he took her place at the counter, she sat on her bed and cried. The widow arrived again that day, having already heard about her lover's fate. She carried with her clothes and the few possessions she owned and that very day replaced the baker, for the bread still had to be made.

For three nights the girl dreamed of the wild hare that had once spoken to her. It said nothing in the dream, just looked at her and bounded away into the forest, towards the hillock that had once been her home. On the fourth night after her father's disappearance, she tiptoed passed the sleeping widow and slipped away into the darkness. Like everything else in the town since the arrival of the dragon, sections of the wall had fallen into disrepair, so finding cracks to squeeze through was not difficult. Outside the walls the hare waited for her. She followed it back to the hillock in the forest.

Now the hare spoke:

"Take the salt from the cave. Fill your skirt with it and return for six more nights with an empty flour bag."

She did as the hare requested, but the full bags were heavy. She had to drag them back to town, and even though the accompanying hare filled her with courage, she could not resist searching the sky for the dragon. But she made it safely back to the shop each night and secured the bags of salt behind the few remaining bags of flour. On the eighth day, she revealed to the widow what the additional bags contained.

"Taste it," she said.

The widow shrugged and placed a crystal on her tongue. She immediately spat it out and gulped a mug of plum wine.

"It's in the bread," the widow said. "From your arms..."

"Yes," the girl replied.

The widow took another crystal and touched it with her tongue.

"It tastes, it tastes..."

"It tastes like thirst," the girl finished.

The two set to work. They baked the largest loafs the ovens could handle, and once they were cool, they scooped out the soft flesh inside and stuffed the remaining shells with the crystals. They labored through the night, and when morning came, they had seven of the largest loaves they had ever seen.

They looked proudly at their work, but how would they get the dragon to eat the bread? As they pondered this, the blacksmith's wife knocked on the shutters. As she stood waiting for her daily ration, she grimaced and grabbed her side.

The widow smiled.

"The bread needs one more ingredient."

And so on that day, the bread was bartered for the rags used by the women in the town for the cycle blood. These the widow and the girl stuffed into the seven loaves.

As far as anyone knew, the dragon ate but once a day. At the high sun, news that a woodcutter had become the dragon's latest victim reached the bakery. When the sun began to set, the girl and the widow dragged the loaves through the trampled hay and manure out into the very middle of the square. With the bread they formed a semblance of a man: two loaves for the torso, four its legs and arms, and one the head. They connected the pieces with strips of raw dough, baking the strips with a burning log. They then draped the bread-man with the old clothes of the baker.

Meanwhile, the townspeople looked out their doors and shook their heads. Did the widow and girl think the dragon could be weaned from its taste of human flesh with bread? Still, the townspeople, desperate for any plan at all, listened to the two bakers when they urged them to stay indoors the next day. Other messengers were sent throughout the town. Many people reminded the messengers of what had happened in the past when the dragon found no one in the open streets; it simply tore the roof off the nearest cottage and grabbed the first body in sight.

One day, the messengers pleaded. You could die in your own home as easily as you could in the square. The townspeople nodded and eventually relented. They ate only half their evening bread, saving the rest for the next day.

When dawn broke the next morning, the wait began. For the first time in weeks no one knocked on the shutters for bread. The bread-man alone occupied the square. Every time the sun passed behind a cloud, throwing a shadow on the ground, the girl and the widow sucked in their breath and grew stiff. They endured so many false starts that they did not even notice the presence of the dragon until it had landed, fifty paces in front of their shop. It gave its wings a feeble flap and yawned.

The dragon did not take its meal immediately. Perhaps the beast was used to catching its prey on the fly. It looked lazily around the square before straightening its serpentine neck so that its nostrils were inches from the bread-man's head. A growl escaped its mouth then. The girl and the widow sucked in their breath once again, for they believed the dragon had discovered the hoax. But with one quick snap of its jaws, the beast ripped away the head and swallowed it whole. With barely a pause, it tore into the body, and within seconds all that remained were the old baker's clothes. The dragon flapped its wings again, and as their speed increased, bits of hay and manure sprayed the surrounding cottages. The beast lifted its body from the ground, rising gradually above the rooftops, before it circled the square three times. As it spiraled up to the sun, all could see that the dragon seemed slow and sluggish. It suddenly stopped in mid-air and craned its neck, releasing a cry from its mouth that rattled the walls of the town.

Its mouth opened wide, the scream still emanating from deep within its body, the dragon dove, but this time beyond the walls and toward the river. Right before the dragon's cry cut off, a sound like a hundred trees crashing to the ground at once hit the ears of the townspeople. A moment later, a curtain of water surged over the town walls and into the square.

...

By the time the Girl with Crystal Arms lay on her deathbed, all that lived in the town during the time of the dragon had passed on. The world around her had changed completely. The town grew rich from the salt trade. What was once a small town of wood and thatch became Cracow, a great city of stone. Soon a king replaced the wisest elder, and a priest replaced the priestess. People continued to tell the story of the dragon, especially when the river, made fast with snowmelt, heaved and growled. As the story was retold and retold, however, the girl was replaced by a very clever boy, for in this new world no one was ready to believe that girls or widows could combat monsters. The girl's observance that the dragon came not from the ground or from the sky, but was of this plane, from the east, was lost to time. In her final moments before sliding into death, she had one last vision: the dragon would one day return, bigger and stronger, and this time it would be joined by another from the west.

THE AUTHOR

Mark Lewandowski is the author of the story collection, *Halibut Rodeo*. His essays, stories, and scripts have appeared in many journals, including *The Gettysburg Review*, *The North American Review*, and *The Florida Review*. In addition to numerous Best of the Net and Pushcart nominations, his work has been listed as "Notable" in *The Best American Essays*, *The Best American Travel Writing*, and *The Best American Nonrequired Writing*. He has taught English as a Peace Corps Volunteer in Poland, and as a Fulbright Scholar in Lithuania. Currently, he is a Professor of English at Indiana State University.